W9-AVA-062

J
DUNLOP, Eileen
The ghost by the sea

DATE DUE

NOV 1 8 2014	

THE GHOST
BY THE SEA

THE GHOST
BY THE SEA

Eileen Dunlop

Holiday House / New York

Library of Congress Cataloging-in-Publication Data
Dunlop, Eileen.
The ghost by the sea / Eileen Dunlop.— 1st ed.
p.   cm.
Summary: While visiting her grandmother who lives alone at
Culaloe, ten-year-old Robin becomes involved in a duel with the
ghost of her great-great-aunt.
ISBN 0-8234-1264-4 (alk. paper)
[1. Ghosts—Fiction,   2. Family life—Scotland—Fiction.
3. Scotland—Fiction.]   I. Title.
PZ7.D9214Gh   1996   96-7271   CIP   AC
[Fic]—dc20

For Betty Sturrock

THE LAMBERTS OF CULALOE

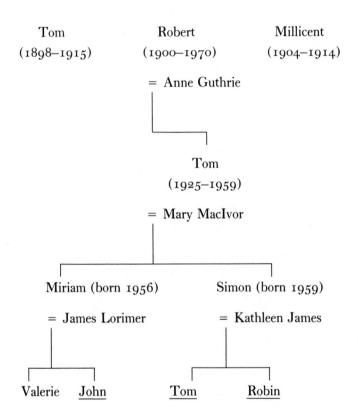

Tom
(1898–1915)

Robert
(1900–1970)

Millicent
(1904–1914)

= Anne Guthrie

Tom
(1925–1959)

= Mary MacIvor

Miriam (born 1956)

= James Lorimer

Simon (born 1959)

= Kathleen James

Valerie   John

Tom   Robin

CONTENTS

1 Mr Grumpus

Only a few hours after Robin had found the old teddy bear in the attic, she heard another child crying as if her heart would break. The noise woke her, drowning the murmur of the sea, rising above the wind that sang around the chimneys of the tall house on the quay. In the darkness Robin listened to the desolate weeping until she could no longer bear it. Clutching the teddy to her chest, she burrowed under the duvet, desperate to shut out the sound of someone else's grief.

The clock on the landing had struck three before the sobbing subsided and Robin again drifted into sleep. When she next woke, she didn't immediately recall what she had heard. As she focussed her eyes on the tiny grey window-panes stamped on the dark wall by the dawn, it was the memory of the previous day that flooded her mind. While daylight strengthened and the shapes of unfamiliar furniture loomed in her little room, Robin lay with the teddy in the crook of her arm and relived yesterday.

It must now be twenty-four hours, she reckoned, since she had hugged Mum in the cold northern morning and got into the car with Dad. As the

mountains had fallen behind on the long road south
from Inverness, her father had scarcely spoken, but
that didn't surprise Robin. Since Christmas Eve,
when her brother Tom had been run down by a van
in the street outside their house, conversation with
Dad had been impossible. Sometimes Robin wondered if he would ever talk to her normally again.

They had stopped for coffee at a service station
outside Dundee, before crossing the windy concrete
bridge over the River Tay. Driving in silence
through the intimate farmlands of Fife, Robin had
watched white seagulls swooping over the ribbed
brown fields, and had sensed the sea before she saw
it glinting behind the black line of the shore.

Granny Lambert's house was called Culaloe. It
was thin and high, with rows of tiny windows set
deeply in its whitewashed walls. Culaloe stood op-
posite the harbour in Sandhaven, a fishing village of
cobbled streets and red-roofed buildings huddling
for shelter in a cove. As she had got out of the car,
Robin had tasted salt on the fine rain spinning out of
a pearly sky.

Dad had refused to stay for lunch, although he
hadn't seen his mother for nearly two years.

"I'm losing time from work, and time's money,"
he had said sharply, as if it were Granny's fault.

But Robin knew that he was really impatient to
get home in case there had been a call from the
hospital to say that Tom was emerging from his
coma — or had taken a turn for the worse. She had

stood at the door, watching the car bumping slowly along the waterfront and turning into the steep alley leading to the main road. She hadn't even pretended that she was sorry to see Dad go. Yet as she found her way back to the unfamiliar kitchen, she couldn't help a slight qualm at the prospect of spending five weeks alone with a woman whom, although she was her grandmother, she scarcely knew.

The day had passed pleasantly enough, however. Granny Lambert, a tall, brown-eyed woman with unruly grey hair and dark, unfashionable clothes, hadn't changed at all since her one and only visit to Robin's family in Inverness. Then she had been polite, but she hadn't made the special effort to be friendly which children expect of strangers. She hadn't brought lavish presents or bought ice cream. She hadn't even asked Tom and Robin what they wanted to be when they grew up. At first the children had found her offhandedness disconcerting, but they soon decided that they liked it.

"She's honest, and it's nice being treated as an adult," said Tom, who had had his tenth birthday a week before Granny Lambert had arrived.

Robin, eighteen months younger, had agreed. Which was why, when Granny Lambert had written offering to have her for an extended Easter holiday, she had said she wanted to go. She had gone on saying so while Mum banged about, sniffing and muttering that Granny Lambert was a bit late with her invitation.

"Honestly, Simon," Mum had said tearfully. "When I think of all the summers when Tom would have loved a seaside holiday, and your mother never once suggested it!"

"It's just like Mother," snapped Dad, for once roused from his misery to give an opinion. " 'Mary, Mary, quite contrary'. Of course, we'll refuse."

"I want to go," Robin had said stubbornly, and had gone on saying so while grenades of resentment against Granny Lambert exploded around her. In the end, because they had more pressing problems, her parents had given in.

"Only don't blame us if you have a miserable time," Mum had warned, apparently unaware that for Robin nothing could possibly be more miserable than life at home just then.

At Sandhaven, Granny was exactly as Robin remembered her in Inverness, pleasant but not effusive.

"I have work to do," she had said after lunch. "Go where you like and do what you like, but don't fall into the harbour. If you want me, I'll be in the pottery at the end of the garden."

Robin had watched her putting plates and cutlery into the dishwasher and tying a dusty apron over her long brown dress. Nodding to Robin, she had gone out through the back door into a narrow, shrubby garden. Robin, who had remembered vaguely hearing pottery referred to at home as Granny's hobby, had watched her striding down an overgrown path and disappearing into a small cottage built against a sandstone wall.

Because by that time it was raining heavily, Robin had spent the afternoon exploring Culaloe. She had climbed steep stairs, groped along dark passages and peeped into tiny rooms crammed with old-fashioned furniture. All the windows were open; the breeze puffed white lace curtains like small sails and carried indoors the sharp air of the sea.

The old house was full of a nautical past — a child's yacht on a windowsill, a painting of a fishing boat called the *Highland Mary*, a model of a light-house under a glass dome. It had seemed to Robin a very large house for one elderly woman, but fading sepia photographs of children in the sailor suits and lace-trimmed frocks of long ago reminded her that Culaloe had once been home to a large family.

Robin found Culaloe interesting, mainly because it was so different from the sparsely furnished modern house where she had lived all her life. But not until she had reached the very top did she find something that delighted her.

The attic at Culaloe contained two small rooms and a long, tent-shaped loft, dimly lit by four cobwebby skylights. Ancient fishing nets still drooped from the rafters under the rattling tiles, giving off a musty, seaweedy smell. Here among dusty trunks and fish-crates, wedged between an empty birdcage and a pile of faded magazines, was a teddy bear sitting on a little wicker chair. His once golden fur was badly worn, but he had bright amber eyes and a gently smiling mouth. When Robin had picked him up and cuddled him, he felt damp, so she had carried him downstairs and perched him on the radiator in her bedroom. Then she had lain on her bed for a while, reading a comic and keeping an eye on him to make sure that he wouldn't singe.

In the evening, after a supper of bacon sandwiches eaten by the kitchen fire, Robin had fetched the teddy and shown him to Granny.

"Does he have a name?" she had inquired.

Granny had taken the old bear and turned him over in her long hands, smiling the way grown-ups do when a toy reminds them of childhood long ago.

"It's Mr Grumpus," she had said.

Robin had watched Granny tickling the teddy's ears and scratching his tummy with her clay-rimmed nails. She obviously knew Mr Grumpus well, but when Robin asked, "Do you know who he belonged to?" she had shrugged her shoulders slightly.

"Lots of people have had a share of him," she had said. "He lived here long before I came to Culaloe. He must be more than ninety years old."

"May I have him?" Robin had asked eagerly, expecting Granny to nod and say, "Of course you may."

She had been disappointed when Granny handed the teddy back to her, saying, "He'll be yours while you're staying at Culaloe."

Robin had wanted to point out that since there

weren't any other children at Culaloe now, there was no reason why she shouldn't have Mr Grumpus to keep. But she didn't know Granny well enough to argue, so she had said no more.

The evening had ended harmoniously with cups of hot chocolate, and at nine o'clock Robin had taken Mr Grumpus and gone upstairs.

In the bath and getting ready for bed, she had felt quite cheerful; after all, she had five weeks in which to persuade Granny to let her keep the bear. As she tucked him under the duvet, she had whispered into his tattered ear, "You're mine now, for ever. Aren't you, Mr Grumpus?"

Mr Grumpus smiled, just as he had smiled at everyone who had ever asked this question. Robin had had no doubt that the smile meant yes.

It was just after ten when she had put out the light. Less than five hours later she heard a child crying in the dark, as if she had lost someone she dearly loved.

2   The Wind and the Sea

Robin was up and half way through getting dressed when she remembered the crying in the night. As she zipped up her jeans and pulled a red jersey over her dark curly head, she felt puzzled but not alarmed. Although with the morning sun shining straight into the room it inevitably occurred to her that she might have been dreaming, she instantly dismissed the idea. In fact, the memory was so un-dreamlike that when she went downstairs to the kitchen, she wouldn't have been surprised to see another girl sitting sullen and red-eyed at the table. However, Granny was alone, and when she said, "Good morning. Did you sleep well?" Robin told her the truth.

"I went to sleep straight away," she said, "but a noise woke me. It was someone crying — upstairs, I think."

Granny was standing at the window with her back to Robin, watching the birds skirmishing over some bread and nuts she had just thrown out for them. Robin was surprised to see her thin shoulders stiffen and to glimpse, when Granny turned round, a shocked expression in her dark eyes. Granny recovered quickly, but she didn't look straight at Robin as she replied.

"It would be the wind and the sea you heard, my dear," she said. "This old house is full of their voices. You'll get used to them soon." And before Robin could answer, she opened a door and went into the pantry to fetch the milk.

Robin sat down at the table, frowning with bewilderment. For a wild moment, she wondered whether Granny had kidnapped someone and was holding her prisoner. But she knew the idea was ridiculous. Yesterday, at Granny's invitation, she had poked her nose into every room in the house. Not one had been locked. As she took the top off her boiled egg and spread butter on a slice of toast, Robin told herself to stop being silly. Of course Granny was right. It was hard to believe, just the same.

While Robin was eating her breakfast, Granny drank coffee and read the newspaper. Her austere face was expressionless and her dark eyes gave nothing away. When Robin had finished, Granny folded up the paper and said, "I have to go to St Andrews this morning to deliver some of my pottery to a shop. Would you like to come?"

Robin was surprised to learn that Granny's hobby produced things good enough to sell, but she nodded and said, "Yes, please."

She had been wondering how best to fill the long day ahead of her.

She ran upstairs to put on her coat and boots. When she came down, Granny had parked her blue van at the front door. While she loaded it with plates, jugs, and bowls jacketed with straw, Robin ran across the quay to look at the harbour. It was quiet and almost deserted, apart from three fishermen unloading their catch from a boat named the *Jenny Spinner* and a gaggle of seagulls waiting hopefully for scraps. It was a picturesque harbour with its lobster cages and piles of green and orange nets, so it displeased Robin to see nearby a tumbledown wharf dominated by a vast and ugly steel crane. Offshore, filthy barges rode at anchor, spoiling the view out to sea.

"What's happening there?" Robin asked Granny, as they drove past and headed uphill towards the main road.

"They're dredging the old harbour," Granny told her. "It hasn't been used since the fishing industry here declined after World War II. But now a development company hopes to open it up again. They're going to build a hotel and a marina, and put Sandhaven on the tourist map." She didn't sound as if the idea appealed to her, but then she laughed and added, "Of course, they have to get rid of the mud first. They've taken out tons already, but there's always more to come."

"It's a mess," said Robin, wrinkling her nose in disgust.

"It's worse when the tide's out," Granny replied.

Though still vaguely anxious, Robin enjoyed the ride along the winding coast road, with greening winter fields on one side and the restless grey sea on the other. There were hedges like streamers of smoke, and red-tiled cottages by the wayside with names that Robin liked: *Conceres, The Luggy, Kintillo Inn.* Granny didn't talk much more than Dad had yesterday, but whatever she was thinking, her company was easy in a way that his wasn't any more.

In the grey, angular town of St Andrews, Granny parked the van by the beach and went off to attend to her business. Robin found a gift shop and chose postcards to send to her parents and Tom. Of course, Tom wouldn't be able to see his now, but it would be there for him when he came out of his coma.

Firmly Robin banished the thought, *If* he comes out of his coma, and with it the memory of Tom as she had seen him only once, a still white figure with bandaged head, lying in hospital hooked up to the beeping machine which sustained his life. Robin had sobbed with terror, and in the car on the way home she had screamed that she never wanted to see Tom like that again. Mum had said that if it upset her so much, there was no point in her visiting. But Dad had used the word "heartless", and Robin knew she hadn't been forgiven.

While she was waiting for Granny, Robin went down on the sand and walked along beside the swishing, turning tide. She closed her eyes, listening intently to the sea's voice and the bluster of the east wind over the waves. But try as she might, she couldn't make them sound like a child crying in the dark. It was difficult to believe that Granny could either.

Running back to the van, Robin decided that in the evening she would mention the matter again. She was convinced that Granny was hiding something, and she wanted to know what, and why. It hadn't even occurred to her yet that there might not be a rational explanation for what she had heard.

3 A Ghost Story

As things turned out, Robin didn't have to wait until evening for an explanation, although it wasn't Granny who provided it. When they got back from St Andrews, Granny cooked omelettes while Robin went upstairs to make her bed and tidy her room. It was a pleasant place with its high, old-fashioned brass bed, polished chest of drawers and faded watercolours of children building sand castles by the sea. Robin propped Mr Grumpus against the pale blue pillow, thinking how well he would look on her pink bed at home.

During lunch, Granny read a book. Obviously she had formed this habit while living alone and saw no reason to alter it now that she had company. As soon as she had finished eating, she made herself a cup of coffee and again put on her apron. She dealt rather brusquely with Robin's heavy hinting that she would like to try her hand at pottery, too.

"There's a potter's wheel at our school, but you're not allowed to use it till you're twelve," Robin remarked.

"And you're not allowed to use mine till you're twenty," retorted Granny. But then she looked at

Robin's disappointed face and added more kindly, "I'm sorry. I have such a lot of work to do just now. I'm late with plates for a wedding present, and I'm having an exhibition which opens in two weeks' time. After that I shan't be so busy, and we'll do things together, I promise."

Left alone in the kitchen, Robin felt lonely for the first time since her arrival. It would have been so different if Tom had been there with her; they could have fished in the rock-pools along the coast, or explored the village together, ending up at the ice cream shop as they always did. On her own, with no one to talk to, being at the seaside wouldn't be half as much fun. Robin spent a few minutes admiring Granny's beautiful sea-blue and sea-green ceramic plates on the dresser, wondering whether to go out or stay in. A burst of rain against the window made up her mind for her; at the same time she remembered that last night she'd noticed a shelf of books in her bedroom.

The books were very old and well read, with rubbed gold spines and titles that Robin had found enticing: *The Garden behind the Moon, Rebecca of Sunnybrook Farm, The Tapestry Room.* She had selected a book and put it on her bedside table, but when she got into bed she hadn't been able to keep her eyes open. Now, with the weather thickening outside, she thought she might as well spend the afternoon reading by the kitchen fire.

Just as she was about to go upstairs to fetch the book, however, the window was momentarily darkened by a passing figure. The garden door was pushed open, and to Robin's surprise, a boy of about twelve, with dark hair very like her own, came into the kitchen. He was wearing faded jeans and a black sweatshirt under a grey waterproof jacket, and he looked across the room with blue eyes that reminded Robin achingly of Tom's.

"You'll be the Lambert girl," said the boy.

Robin nodded. "I'm Robin," she said. "Who are you?"

"John Lorimer." The boy put a plastic carrier bag on the pine table. "I've brought the eggs for Granny," he said, then laughed as he noticed Robin's mystified expression. "You've never heard of me, have you?" he asked.

"No," admitted Robin.

It had never even crossed her mind that Granny might have grandchildren other than Tom and herself. Although this boy was obviously related, she couldn't place him at all. John Lorimer shrugged off his wet jacket and slung it over a wooden chair. Then he sat down in Granny's armchair, holding out strong red hands to the fire.

"I'm not surprised," he said. "Your dad and my mum fell out years ago — don't ask me why — but they're brother and sister, so we're cousins. It's a wonder Granny didn't tell you about me, though." For a moment John looked slightly piqued by this omission, but then he laughed. "Or on second thoughts, not a wonder," he concluded.

Despite her astonishment, Robin grinned. She

liked this unexpected cousin who had eyes like Tom's and seemed friendly towards her, whatever the quarrel between their parents might be. "Is Granny absentminded, then?" she asked.

John took a moment to consider this.

"She isn't forgetful," he said. "At least, not more than other old people. But if something's upset her — like our parents falling out — she won't ever talk about it. I knew about you from Mum, but I'd never heard Granny mention you, until . . ."

"Until when?"

"Until she came to tell Mum about your brother. She thought Mum should know," replied John. "Sorry, by the way. Is he —"

"Just the same," said Robin. Then, because she didn't want to talk about Tom, she went on quickly, "Do you live in Sandhaven, John?"

"No. My dad farms at Clunybank, out the Tarvit road." John took a log from a basket beside the hearth and put it on the fire. He kicked it with the sole of his boot, making an eruption of orange sparks. Then he leant back in his chair and stared at Robin with his bright blue eyes. "I wouldn't mind living in Sandhaven," he told her. "I like the harbour. But I don't think I'd like to live at Culaloe."

"Why not?"

"Because it's haunted."

For the life of her, Robin couldn't decide whether the boy was serious. Silently she returned John's gaze, trying to detect a glimmer of mischief or a slight twitch of the lips that would tell her he was only trying to scare her. At last she said sceptically, "Oh, yes? Who by?"

"A girl," replied John. "About your age, probably. Her name was Milly Lambert and she died in a boating accident, away back before World War I. She must have been — let me see — our great-great-aunt. Granny's husband was her nephew."

"Who's actually seen her?" inquired Robin, still very cool.

Later she would think she had been incredibly slow to make the vital connection, but at this point she still wasn't alarmed. Life with teasing Tom had made her suspicious of twelve-year-old male jokers, and she was determined not to give John Lorimer the satisfaction of thinking he had scared her. For the very last time in her life, Robin told herself that there was no such thing as a ghost. John shrugged his shoulders.

"I don't know who's *seen* her," he said, "but when my mum lived here long ago, she sometimes heard her running about upstairs and singing.

> *Stockings red, garters blue,*
> *Trimmed all round with silver,*
> *A rose so red upon my head*
> *And a gold ring on my finger.*

John made his voice high like a little girl's, but Robin wasn't laughing. "And sometimes she cried

in the night, and called out that she wanted Tom,"
he said.

Robin felt her heart thudding against her ribs.
The truth was so obvious now, she couldn't imagine
how she had ever thought that the sobbing child
was human. She had a horrible sensation, as if cold,
damp fingers were stroking her cheeks. She had
to swallow hard before she managed to whisper,
"Tom?"

"Her brother. Our great-great-uncle. He was in
the boat with her when she drowned."

Too shocked to speak, Robin stared incredulously
at John Lorimer. But even if she had been able or
had wanted to tell him that she, too, had heard Milly
Lambert crying in the night, she didn't have time.
Unnoticed by the two children, the garden door had
swung half open as Granny paused on the doorstep
to take off her wet shoes. A moment later it almost
parted from its hinges as she thrust it wide open and
whirled into the kitchen. Her cheeks were flushed
and her dark eyes blazed with anger.

"You horrible boy, John Lorimer," she almost
spat at her grandson. "Wasn't it only two days ago I
warned you to hold your tongue and not go frightening Robin? Get away home this minute, and don't
dare to come back here unless you're invited."

Briefly John attempted defiance.

"You haven't paid for the eggs," he said.

But then he took one look at Granny's face,
jumped out of the chair, grabbed his jacket and

bolted. As his footsteps thudded away along the garden path, Granny and Robin looked unhappily at each other.

"It's true, isn't it?" quavered Robin.

Granny sighed deeply. Her anger had fallen away suddenly, leaving her pale and tired.

"Yes," she said.

4 Family Matters

For the rest of that day, Granny behaved for the first time in a normal, granny-like way.

"We'll talk about this in the evening," she said gently, and with an apparent change of heart, she led Robin through the garden to the little cottage she used as a studio.

At another time Robin would have loved the place, with its dusty shelves crammed with plates and bowls, some biscuit-fired and some already painted in all the colours of the sea. She would have enjoyed the clutter of paints and glazes and jam-jars full of brushes and modelling tools, and sniffed appreciatively the earthy smell of clay. But now fear blurred her eyes and muffled her other senses.

When Granny had tied an apron round Robin and given her a clay-board and a lump of wet clay, she sat down and resumed painting silver starfish on the rim of a large turquoise plate. Robin sat at a scarred old table by the window, her hands automatically rolling the long clay sausages she needed to make a coil pot. But her mind was elsewhere. As she stared across the turbulent, shadowy garden at the soft light shining from the kitchen window, the awfulness of her position almost made her choke. Culaloe was a haunted house. Robin didn't know how she would ever dare to enter it again.

At half-past five, however, when Granny had tidied her bench and put out the studio light, Robin took her outstretched hand and walked beside her through the dark, windswept garden. Somehow strength seemed to be transmitted through Granny's fingers, and it wasn't so difficult to step through the door into the warm kitchen.

While Granny made salad and put two potatoes into the oven to bake, Robin laid the table and even managed a quick dash to the bathroom across the hall. She tried not to think about the warren of blind passages and rooms piled above her, telling herself sternly to take one thing at a time. To her surprise, she enjoyed her supper, and by the time she and Granny were settled with their coffee by the fire, she had recovered enough to listen to the story Granny had to tell.

"I can't really explain," admitted Granny candidly. "I've lived in this house for nearly forty years, and having a ghost upstairs is still as strange to me as it is to you. But I can tell you about her, and perhaps when you know what happened you'll feel more sorry for her than afraid."

Robin doubted this, but she said, "Please go on."

Granny drank some coffee and took a few moments to arrange her thoughts. Then she said, "There have been Lamberts at Culaloe ever since the house was built in 1780. In every generation it has been the custom to call the eldest son Tom. My husband, your grandfather Tom Lambert, was the only son of Robert Lambert, who was born in 1900. Robert had an elder brother, Tom, born in 1898, and a younger sister Millicent, born in 1904."

"Milly. The ghost," said Robin.

"Yes." Granny leaned forward to poke the fire, making blue and orange flames reach for the chimney. "I'm afraid," she continued, "that Milly wasn't a nice child. She was doted on by her parents and terribly spoilt by her brother Tom. To be fair, Milly adored him, too, but otherwise she was spiteful and famous for her fits of rage. Her other brother, Robert, suffered most. Milly was jealous and did all she could to prevent his being friends with Tom." Granny's dark eyes stared sadly into the past. "Poor children," she sighed. "Such a pity they couldn't just have enjoyed each other's company. Their time together was so short."

"John told me that Milly drowned," Robin said.

Granny nodded.

"A century ago the fishing industry was flourishing, and the Lamberts were quite wealthy people. Tom had a boat of his own, a one-masted dinghy he called the *Milly Dear*. One afternoon in June 1914, when he was sixteen and Milly was ten, they went for a picnic to Barns Island — no great distance. You can see it from your bedroom window."

Robin had noticed the rocky islet, like an elephant's back rising out of the sea.

"And?" she prompted.

"It was a lovely clear day when they set out," Granny told her, "but suddenly a thick fog — what we call a haar on this coast — rolled in from the sea. I can't tell you what happened, because with such poor visibility there were no witnesses and Tom Lambert never told anyone. But although the sea was as calm as a pond, the *Milly Dear* overturned at the entrance to the old harbour and sank. Milly went down with it. Her body was washed up on the shore at Kinghorn three weeks later, and was buried in St Fillan's churchyard. Her spirit came back to Cula-loe."

In spite of the fire's warmth, Robin couldn't repress a shiver at this plain statement. The story was fascinating, all the same.

"What happened to Tom?" she asked.

"Tom swam to the breakwater and hoisted himself out of the water by some iron rungs," said Granny. "Neither his parents nor the police who investigated the accident could get him to explain, and I'm afraid everyone thought he was a coward who had saved himself and let his little sister drown."

"Poor Tom," whispered Robin.

"Yes." Granny gave her an approving look. "I've always felt sorry for him, too. However, two months later World War I broke out. Tom enlisted immediately, although he was under age. In 1915, just after they had received a letter from him saying that he would never come back to Sandhaven, his parents were informed that he had gone missing in battle and was presumed dead."

"Was he?" asked Robin. "Dead, I mean?"

Granny shrugged slightly. "I suppose so," she said. "I believe his mother wrote several times to the War Office in London asking for more details but got very little response. Fifty thousand British lives were lost in the battle Tom was fighting, so the fate of one soldier was of no importance to anyone except his family. Whatever happened, he was never heard of again."

Robin heard anger as well as sadness in Granny's voice, but World War I was distant history to her. In her eagerness to hear more about Milly, she brushed its tragedy aside.

"You said that Milly's spirit came back to Culaloe," she reminded Granny. "Who saw it?"

"Her own father first," Granny said. "He was quite old to have such young children, and he never got over tragedy striking two of them. Just after Tom left home he had a stroke, and although he recovered his speech he was never out of bed again. Towards the end of his life he kept telling his son Robert that Milly was in the room. Robert thought the old man was hallucinating."

"Didn't Robert see her?"

"No." Granny shook her head. "Although she'd been such a pest to him in life, Milly didn't haunt Robert. It wasn't until he had a son of his own — the Tom Lambert who was my husband and your grandfather — that Robert was forced to accept that Milly was still at Culaloe."

"How come?" asked Robin, her dark eyes wide in the firelight.

"Little Tom kept on prattling about the girl who lived upstairs," said Granny. "At first Robert tried to believe that the child had an imaginary friend, as many small children do. But then one day he heard Tom singing in the garden:

> *Stockings red, garters blue,*
> *Trimmed all round with silver,*
> *A rose so red upon my head*
> *And a gold ring on my finger.*

"It's just an old schoolyard rhyme, but Milly loved it and in the family it was known as 'Milly's song'. Only little Tom had never been told about Milly."

Again Robin shivered, but she said nothing and Granny continued calmly.

"Your grandfather was haunted by Milly all his life. But he died long ago, and in recent years you'd hardly have known she was here at all. Your father never saw or heard her and doesn't believe that she exists. My daughter Miriam never saw Milly, but sometimes she heard her singing — and crying in the night, as you did."

"Yes. John told me that." Robin nodded, but mention of her father had made her think of something else. "Granny," she said, "if the eldest Lambert son is always called Tom, how come my dad is called Simon?"

For the first time, Granny shifted uneasily in her chair, and Robin sensed reluctance to look her in the eye. Yet the explanation seemed honest enough.

"Nearly forty years ago," she said, "my husband was drowned when his fishing boat sank in a terrible storm. We had been married for only four years. Miriam was barely three and your father wasn't born until six weeks later. Let's just say I didn't think 'Tom' was a happy name. I wanted my son to have a new name and a fresh start."

"I understand," Robin said. But then she blurted out, "What I don't understand is how you could bear to live all these years in a haunted house."

Granny looked startled, but then she said simply, "I've never wanted to live anywhere else. I love this house, and all my life I've been under the spell of the sea. If the ghost had troubled my children I'd have left, of course, but she didn't. She's never troubled me, either."

"Have you never even heard her?"

"No, never," said Granny, but when Robin opened her mouth to ask another question, she firmly cut her short.

"The point is, Robin, that you don't have to live in a haunted house. I can see I made a mistake in asking you to come here, and I'm sorry. You can sleep in my room tonight, and in the morning I'll telephone your parents. If I drive you to Perth and put you on the afternoon train, they'll meet you in Inverness."

Robin was completely taken aback. Even at the height of her panic in the studio, she hadn't considered going home. Now the memory of the stricken household she'd been so eager to leave swept through her mind; the tetchy atmosphere, the terror every time the telephone rang, her own terrible sense of guilt because the accident hadn't happened to her. She remembered Tom's empty bedroom, with his silent computer and furry cat pyjama-holder grinning inappropriately on the bed. Then Robin thought of cheeky John Lorimer, and Aunt Miriam and the farm she was longing to see. She thought of the peace which, ghost or no ghost, she was finding in Granny's company.

"Granny, please don't," she cried. "I want to stay, really I do."

Granny's smile transformed her tired face. But, "I'm so glad," was all she said as she got up and went to fill the kettle. After she had switched it on, she looked seriously at Robin.

"I know it must be difficult to discover that you're sharing a house with a ghost," she said. "But honestly, I don't think you should be afraid. I have very good reason to believe that Milly Lambert is no danger to any little girl. If I hadn't, do you suppose I'd have risked inviting you here?"

5   A Letter from the Past

That night Robin slept deeply and dreamlessly. She had had butterflies in her tummy before going upstairs, but her bedtime hot chocolate had soothed her and there were no scary moments. Granny had stayed nearby and when Robin was in bed she had come to tuck her in.

"My room's just across the passage from yours," she had said reassuringly. "I'll leave both doors open. If you want me, you only have to call."

But Robin hadn't had to call. Exhausted by over-excitement, she had hugged Mr Grumpus and immediately fallen asleep.

The clock on the landing was striking seven when Robin awoke next morning to find dawn poking faint fingers into the little white-walled room. As was usual when she first awakened, she didn't immediately remember what had happened yesterday. Since there was no sound or movement in Granny's room, she did automatically what she always did at home if she woke early. Rolling over, she switched on the bedside lamp and picked up her book. It was pleasant having a quiet read before the stir of the day began.

The book which Robin had chosen was called *The Red Fox*. She liked its faded but still beautiful russet binding, stamped with gilt lettering and a fox in scarlet and gold. But when she flipped back the front cover, a shock awaited her. Yesterday's events returned in a vivid flash as she saw, written on the flyleaf in faded ink, "To Milly. Much love on your ninth birthday from Tom. 10 January 1913." Robin dropped the book as if it had stung her hand.

Suppose, she thought with a returning thrill of nervousness, that this was Milly Lambert's room. Suppose even that she was sleeping in Milly Lambert's bed! Robin was only saved from total panic by the sound of Granny's mattress exhaling as she got out of bed. A moment later she appeared in her blue dressing gown, her grey hair like a bird's nest that had just survived a storm.

"Good morning. Sleep well?" she asked.

"Yes," Robin replied, but before she had time to ask questions, Granny had gone off to the bathroom.

As she pushed back the duvet, Robin couldn't help wondering whether it wouldn't have been wiser to call it a day here and go home. At breakfast, however, things seemed to take a wonderful turn for the better.

"I've been wondering," said Granny, as she poured the coffee, "whether you'd like me to ask John Lorimer to come and stay with us for a couple of weeks. The school holidays have begun and I dare say his mother would enjoy a holiday from him."

"Brilliant," said Robin delightedly.

She had really liked John, in spite of his teasing, and had been afraid that Granny was too angry with him to allow them to meet again. Granny must have known what Robin was thinking, because she smiled ruefully and added, "I know he's a rascal, but I can never be furious with him for long."

Robin understood and laughed. She still thought there was a snag, however.

"John told me he wouldn't like to stay at Culaloe because it's haunted," she pointed out.

Granny uttered a snorting sound, half of amusement and half of derision. "He's stayed often enough before without suffering nervous collapse," she said dryly. As she lifted the newspaper, she added, "Believe me, Robin. Nothing would frighten that boy. Absolutely nothing."

Bully for him, thought Robin, but all she said was, "Will you telephone the farm?"

"After breakfast," promised Granny, but before she could give her attention to the morning news, Robin had another question for her. After what John had said yesterday about Granny's unwillingness to talk about upsetting things, she was afraid of a curt response, but still she felt she had to ask.

"Granny," she said, "I was wondering. Why did my dad and John's mum fall out?"

Granny put down the paper and looked at Robin over her half-moon glasses. There was some exasperation in her eyes, but Robin was relieved to see amusement, too.

"Dear me," said Granny dryly. "Master Lorimer did spill a lot of beans yesterday, didn't he?" But she must have thought that Robin deserved an explanation, because she went on patiently. "They fell out about the things families usually fall out about, Robin — money and property. Clunybank Farm belonged to my father, John MacIvor. It had been in our family for as long as the Lamberts had owned Culaloe, so it was a great sadness to my father that he had no son to inherit it. I was his only child, and when he realised that I wasn't going to marry a farmer and take over the farm, he was deeply disappointed. When my husband died, I stayed on at Culaloe to keep house for my father-in-law —"

"Milly's brother Robert?"

"Yes. He outlived his son by many years. But I never quarrelled with my own father, and I always took the children to visit him on Saturdays. Simon never showed the least interest in the farm, but Miriam loved it. The minute she left school she went to live with her grandfather at Clunybank, and not long after that she married James Lorimer, the Clunybank dairyman."

"Oh, I see," said Robin, understanding. "So your father gave them the farm."

Granny nodded. "Yes. At least he left it to them when he died. I'm afraid your father got nothing. Of course he'll have Culaloe when I'm dead, but there's really no comparison. Clunybank is worth a fortune. Your father was very angry. He accused Miriam of sucking up to her grandfather deliberately to get the farm, and me of encouraging her. It wasn't true, but I can see why he was upset."

There was a moment's silence. Robin thought of her father, made redundant by the company where he'd worked for eighteen years, and now trying to make ends meet by doing friends' accounts in the spare bedroom at home. Worrying about paying the mortgage and having to tell Tom that he couldn't go on the school trip to France. Dad also never talked about things that upset him, and the measure of his grievance was that he'd never even mentioned his sister to his children.

"It doesn't seem very fair," Robin couldn't help saying, "especially since Tom wants to be a farmer when he grows up."

But Granny responded only to the second part of this remark.

"I suppose farming's in Tom's blood," she said, with a slight, sad shake of her head.

When breakfast was over, Granny suggested that Robin go and make her bed while she tidied the kitchen and telephoned Clunybank Farm. More at ease than she could have imagined an hour earlier, Robin went whistling upstairs. The sight of *The Red Fox* lying on the duvet caused her a slight frisson, but as she made the bed she felt mostly curious. When she had settled Mr Grumpus on the pillow, Robin sat down on the floor and began to examine other books on the shelf.

They were all, she reckoned, about the same age

as *The Red Fox,* and it seemed they had all belonged to Milly Lambert. Robin couldn't help feeling sad as she read the affectionate messages written by people long dead: "To Millicent, with best wishes from Cousin Charlotte." "To Milly Dear. Happy Christmas from Tom." "For Milly, with Papa's love." Robin knew better than most the pain these people must have felt at the loss of a child, and she pitied Milly, who had loved books and had such a short time for reading them.

Robin was glancing at the illustrations in *The Magic Fishbone* but thinking of her own brother Tom when her fingers dislodged a folded piece of paper. Its yellow edges and frailty made Robin withdraw it very carefully. The sheet was splitting along the fold, but the round, childish writing was perfectly clear. Robin read the pencilled words with unease.

5 June 1914

Dear Tom,

Thank you for the postcard from London and the skipping-rope you sent. I can do forty-two skips without stopping. Yesterday Robert gave me some hair ribbons but I threw them on the fire. I hate Robert and I would like to kill him. Please hurry home. I am looking forward to our sail to Barns Island and I am mis —

The letter stopped in the middle of a word, never finished and never sent. Robin would have liked to believe that shame had prevented Milly from sending it, but after what Granny had told her last night, she doubted it. Any feelings of sympathy for Milly faded as she put the paper back in the book. In spite of the morning sunshine the jealous, unkind letter had brought darkness into the room.

Robin got up in a hurry and ran downstairs to the kitchen.

"Granny," she said abruptly, "am I sleeping in Milly Lambert's room?"

Granny, who was watering her houseplants, turned and put her jug down on the table. If she felt surprise, she didn't show it. "No," she said. "In Milly's time the children's rooms were in the attic, so that they didn't disturb the grown-ups downstairs. The room you have was your aunt Miriam's."

"Oh, I see," said Robin. "I just wondered, because Milly's books are there."

"Are they?" Granny sounded vague. "I expect Miriam brought them down. She was always fond of reading. But now" — her voice became brisker — "you must go and put on your outdoor clothes. Your cousin is coming this afternoon, so we'll have to go and stock up with food at the supermarket. Eats like a seagull, that boy does."

6   Burial Hill

John arrived at three o'clock, swooping along the lane behind Culaloe on a bicycle dangerously loaded with a rucksack, tape recorder, and case of cassettes.

"This is magic," he told Robin as he dumped his belongings on the kitchen floor and helped himself to cookies from a box on the dresser. "Mum and Dad are off to a farmers' convention tomorrow, and I was supposed to be going with them. I'd have been bored out of my mind. Now we can have some fun."

"*If* you're not too scared to stay here," Robin couldn't help saying acidly, but when John sniggered she couldn't keep her face straight either. Again she was reminded of Tom, who could always make her laugh when she was trying not to. "I'll help you take your stuff upstairs," she said.

John's quarters were a tiny room at the top of the first flight of stairs, just two doors away from Robin's. It had blue walls and a square window with a view of the garden and red roofs beyond. John slung his rucksack onto the narrow bed, but before he even began to unpack he plugged in his tape recorder and put in a cassette.

35

"Granny just loves my kind of music," he said, as a blast of heavy metal shook the quiet house.

Robin fell about giggling once again.

With John's company, the next three days were the happiest Robin had spent since Tom's accident — so happy, indeed, that she almost forgot the mystery that had shadowed her first hours at Sandhaven. Whatever Granny thought of heavy metal, she was rarely in the house to hear it; she went back to work with an air of relief, emerging from the studio only to cook and argue amicably with John about farming matters. Even if she hadn't wanted to take over Clunybank, she seemed to have strong views on egg production and humane methods of rearing pigs. John didn't mention Milly — Robin guessed on Granny's orders — and it wasn't until late on the Tuesday after her arrival that Robin's attention was again focussed on the tragic events of long ago.

It had been a mild day, serene and spring-like, and the two children had spent it outdoors. In the morning they had watched the fishing boats landing their catch, then strolled along to the old harbour. Much as they disliked the excavation which seemed to be soiling the whole village, both John and Robin were fascinated by the huge crane with its vast iron jaws. Walking out onto the breakwater, they stood watching it gobbling up mouthfuls of black mud and spitting them into a dirty barge. More fascinating still was the pile of objects dredged up and cast aside on the quay: old bicycles, an ancient sewing machine, prams, bits of televisions and cars, even a lamppost. It seemed that for the residents of Sandhaven, the old harbour was a convenient rubbish dump.

In the afternoon, John took Robin to explore the streets and alleys of the village. Some were as narrow as tunnels and some so steep that gables and chimney stacks seemed poised to tumble out of the sky. They stopped off at the village store to buy ice cream, then made a detour to look at a painted wooden mermaid, the figurehead from an old sailing ship, which had found a home among the shrubs in a cottage garden. After five-thirty, when the sun was sinking and mist softening the sky, they turned homeward down a street with a sign saying, *Burial Hill.*

"What an odd name," remarked Robin. But John said, "No, it isn't really." Beckoning her towards a rusty gate in a high wall, he added. "Come on. I want to show you something."

As John pushed back the bolt and the gate creaked open, Robin peered uneasily over his shoulder. At once she understood the street's name. The wall concealed an old graveyard. A small, derelict church squatted at the end of a weedy gravel path, sinister with broken windows and dark, gaping doors. All around, headstones reared from the faded winter grass.

The place was very quiet, and with shadows lengthening and vapour beginning to curl around the stones, Robin was afraid. She wanted to run away, but pride prevented her. When John began to lope across the spongy grass, she gritted her teeth and followed him.

John led Robin to the far side of the church, then stopped suddenly. Robin caught in his eyes the gleam of mischief she'd last seen on the afternoon when he'd told her about Milly's ghost. It dawned on her that he'd brought her here on purpose to scare her, and she was both hurt and furious. But before she could spit out a bitter reproach, John said, "Look at this."

Reluctantly following the direction of his pointing finger, Robin saw a large marble monument built right up against the church wall. The stone was soiled and the carved angel on top defaced by more than eighty years of storms. But the lettering was clear in the amber glow of the setting sun.

IN LOVING MEMORY OF
MILLICENT LAMBERT
WHO WAS DROWNED AT SANDHAVEN
13 JUNE 1914
AGED 10 YEARS

THE LORD GAVE
AND THE LORD HATH TAKEN AWAY

Robin had been chilly before. Now she felt as cold as ice. Staring at Milly's memorial, she imagined the lonely darkness of drowning and remembered with overwhelming pity the little body cast up more than twenty miles away by the indifferent sea. But it was John's whispered words that made her shudder and draw her coat tightly around her.

"Only the Lord didn't take Milly Lambert, did he?"

"I want to go home," sniffed Robin.

It was getting dark as the two cousins made their way back along the waterfront. Red lamps winked at the mastheads and the reflections of the harbour lights shivered in the oily water. For the first time since John's arrival at Culaloe, there was restraint between them. John whistled tunelessly and kicked an empty Coke can along the gutter. Robin walked apart with her shoulders hunched. When they reached home and John went round to the back door, she slipped in at the front. Gloomily she climbed the stair and closed the door of her room firmly behind her.

7 Serious Talk

Supper that night was an unusually silent meal. Robin and John concentrated on their food and avoided each other's eyes. Granny, with her nose in her library book, didn't seem to notice, and Robin couldn't help a slight twinge of resentment. It seemed to her that Granny, having asked John to keep her company, had conveniently forgotten how upsetting her first hours at Culaloe had been.

Robin was slightly mollified towards the end of supper when Granny smiled at her and said, "Is everything all right? What have you been doing to-day?" Then she felt piqued again when John cut through her reply.

"Hey, Granny," he said, "have you seen the junk the crane's yanked out of the old harbour? You don't need a sewing machine, do you, or a bike?"

"No, thanks," Granny replied. "I can't sew and my cycling days are over."

Then she went back to her book, apparently not noticing that her questions to Robin were still un-answered.

After the table was cleared, Granny got out some work she had brought over from the studio. Robin left her sitting at the table with her jars and brushes and went up to her room. A few moments later she heard John come up, then the sound of his feet thudding down again to the shower beside the front door.

Robin, who had bathed earlier, undressed and got into bed with Mr Grumpus. Milly's storybooks had proved too long and full of big words to hold her attention, so she had bought herself a couple of paperbacks at the village store. Pulling the duvet round her ears, she tried to lose herself in one of them, but even concentrating on a simple adventure story was beyond her.

In her imagination she kept returning to Burial Hill and walking again through the desolate graveyard where Milly Lambert's body lay. She was still sore at John, not only because he had scared her once again, but also because the ghostly talk had spoiled the fun they'd been having.

Robin's heart sank when she heard John coming back upstairs. Fervently she willed him to go into his room and stay there. But her instinct was that he wouldn't, and she was right. A moment later she heard his feet in the passage, then his fingers tapping lightly on her door.

"OK if I come in?"

John's damp head appeared first, and before Robin could reply the rest of his body followed. He was wearing blue pyjamas and an old plaid dressing gown that had once belonged to Robin's father; Granny, who disliked waste, now kept it for visiting boys. As she closed her book, Robin thought how old-fashioned it looked compared with Tom's garish, cartoon-decorated nightwear. Immediately she felt a sharp stab of guilt, because this was the first time she'd allowed herself to think about Tom since John had come to stay.

Suddenly a longing for her brother swept over Robin, so intense and burning that her throat contracted and tears pricked behind her eyes. Although they bickered from time to time, she and Tom had always been close friends. He was a kind, easygoing person who never seemed to mind his little sister following him around; he had taught Robin to skateboard, helped her with her homework, and made her giggle when Dad was in a roaring mood.

The thought of life without Tom was unbearable to Robin; since the dreadful day when she had seen him in hospital, she had only been able to cope with her grief and fear by pushing the accident to the back of her mind and concentrating very hard on other things. Staring at John with eyes hot with unshed tears, she realised how brittle the happiness of the last few days had been.

"What do you want?" she demanded as John bounced onto the end of the bed.

The answer was disarming.

"To say I'm sorry. I didn't mean to scare you in the graveyard — well, not so much. I just thought it'd be a bit of a laugh." He caught Robin's eye and couldn't help grinning. "For me anyway. Sorry."

"I'm glad somebody thought it was funny," re-torted Robin, just managing to grin, too.

But John's smile had already faded. Kicking off his slippers, he drew up his feet and turned round so that he was facing Robin.

"I didn't," he said. "At least, only for a minute. When I saw that I'd really frightened you, I realised that Mum's right."

"What about?"

"She says we shouldn't laugh at ghosts. They don't hang around houses saying 'Woo-woo-woo' for fun."

Robin, who had been dreading this conversation, suddenly felt relieved. After all, not talking about Milly Lambert's ghost wasn't going to make it go away. Besides, wasn't it a bit humiliating to know that John had been forbidden to mention Milly be-cause Robin was a baby and easily scared? So she looked straight at him and said resolutely, "OK. So why do they hang around houses?"

John paused, frowning, then said, "Mum reckons they hang around when injustice has been done and there's a wrong to be put right."

Robin remembered that John's mother, her un-known Aunt Miriam, had been used to hearing Milly when she was a child at Culaloe. This was serious talk.

"Such as?" prompted Robin.

"Such as the injustice that was probably done to Milly's brother Tom," replied John soberly. "The

Milly Dear overturned at the harbour mouth on a day when the sea was perfectly calm. Tom Lambert was blamed for capsizing the boat and for not rescuing his little sister. But that doesn't square with his reputation."

Robin had already heard of this incident from Granny, but at the time she had been chiefly interested in Milly. Now she found herself becoming interested in Tom.

"Go on, John," she urged.

John leant forward, hugging his knees.

"When Mum was young," he told Robin, "her grandpa was still living here at Culaloe. He was Robert Lambert, Tom and Milly's brother. Mum remembers him saying that he could never understand the accident, because Tom was an expert sailor and a strong swimmer. He was also very brave, and earlier that year he had risked his life in icy water to save a dog that had fallen into the sea. Old Robert could never believe that Tom was a coward. Besides, he doted on Milly and would never have let her drown if he could help it."

"That's what Granny thinks," Robin told John. They looked at each other in silence for a moment, then Robin helplessly shook her head. "It's very mysterious," she admitted, "but it's all so long ago. I don't think there's anything we can do about it now."

But even as the words were coming out of her mouth, Robin saw a brightening in John's blue eyes. Obviously he had other ideas.

"You're wrong," he said eagerly. "Mysteries can be solved, especially if there are clues left behind. This house is full of the past — photographs and clothes and boxes stuffed with letters and old newspapers. I've often thought I'd like to have a shot at finding out what happened, but when I've stayed here before there've always been grown-ups snooping around. But now, with Granny out in the pottery all day, it's a great opportunity. Come on — what d'you say?"

Looking at his eager face, Robin thought that if he had heard a ghost howling in the night he might not be quite so jaunty. But she couldn't help being moved by what he said next.

"Of course it's too late to make any difference to Tom Lambert now. The poor guy's just a name on the Sandhaven war memorial. But the truth would set the record straight, and if Mum's right, then maybe Milly would be able to rest in peace."

Different feelings conflicted in Robin as she clutched Mr Grumpus and gazed at John. Among them were pity for Tom and a sharing of John's desire that the weeping ghost-child should find peace. She also thought it would be exciting to play detectives with John, and to have an interest which would divert her mind from what was happening at home. Yet the fear of rousing a spiteful spirit made her heart bump uncomfortably, and she very nearly blurted out a refusal. In the end, it was again pride that fortified her. She said yes because she didn't want John Lorimer calling her chicken.

"OK. I'll join in," she said.

"Brilliant," said John.

Robin watched him climb off the bed and grope for his slippers. No amount of looking down and trying to keep his mouth in a straight line could disguise his satisfaction.

"Only Granny won't like it, and I bet Milly won't either," Robin couldn't help squeaking as she realised what she'd let herself in for.

John tutted indifferently. "Granny won't know," he said, "unless we tell her, which I shan't, and I hope you won't either, unless you want to see me plastered all over the kitchen. As for Milly —" He shrugged strong shoulders under the plaid dressing gown. "What's there to worry about? Even if she wasn't a nice kid, there's no evidence that she ever did anyone any harm. We're young and healthy and alive. What could a poor little spook like Milly Lambert do against us?"

Often, during the days that followed, Robin would remember this question, but at the time she had no answer. When John had gone and she'd switched off the light, it was Granny's voice she seemed to hear in the dark.

"Believe me, Robin. Nothing would frighten that boy. Absolutely nothing."

Which might, Robin thought, be because John was abnormally brave. Or it might be because nothing frightening had happened to him yet.

8 The Fish Loft Door

"Promise not to play tricks on me," pleaded Robin next morning, as she and John turned from the third-floor landing onto the steep attic stair. She was half regretting her decision to play detectives, because even in John's company the draughty, ill-lit upper floors of Culaloe were giving her the creeps. It amazed her to think that on her first day here she had roamed happily all over the house — but that was before she had heard of Milly Lambert. "Promise," she repeated sternly.

John, who was ahead of her, turned and grinned. "OK. Promise," he said.

It had been obvious at breakfast that John was all agog to start searching. The minute Granny put on her apron and wandered off through the dripping garden to the studio, he had gone into overdrive.

"Never mind clearing up," he had said impatiently. "We'll start at the top of the house and work our way down. I'm really looking forward to this. Aren't you?"

"Mm," said Robin, noncommittally.

In one of the coast's sudden weather changes, the fine weather had vanished overnight. Now it was wet and windy outside, and indoors it was barely light. Doors rattled in the draught, and the deep stairwell was full of moist shadows. Every time a tread of the old stair creaked, Robin jumped and clutched at the banister. Of course, she tried to tell herself, she was not in any danger. She was hearing rain hitting the roof and the soughing of the wind, not the patter of feet and the sighs of a sad spirit. Yet she knew that Milly was up there somewhere, no less scary for being unseen. By the time she and John reached the tiny landing at the top of the attic stair, Robin felt like a coiled spring ready to snap.

"We'll look in the fish loft first, shall we?" said John, turning the handle on the nearest of three narrow doors.

"If you like," Robin said.

The place John called the fish loft was even gloomier in the morning than on the afternoon when Robin had found Mr Grumpus, but John's fingers found a light switch just inside the door. Four electric bulbs flicked on at the apex of the roof, casting apathetic light on drifting cobwebs and the tired old fishing nets. It was like a scene from a horror movie, and Robin couldn't help shuddering as she stepped inside. Suppose, she thought, biting her thumbnail, that Milly Lambert suddenly leapt out on her from the shadows? Surely I would die of fright?

John wasn't troubled by such thoughts, apparently. Carelessly he kicked a dusty path among the nets and piles of trash that hardly seemed worth the trouble of lugging to the top of the house.

"Granny keeps saying she's going to have this place cleared out," he remarked, "then excuses herself because of her rheumaticky knees. I don't think we'll find much here."

Robin, peering at dusty lobster pots, old garden furniture and ancient luggage, agreed. Halfheartedly she opened a suitcase and squealed when a mouse shot out and disappeared under an old kitchen dresser. The place was absolutely freezing, and when John began to push his way back to the door, Robin couldn't follow fast enough. Halfway down the fish loft, however, she noticed something puzzling.

"Just a minute," she said.

"Have you found something?"

John turned back eagerly, but Robin shook her head. She was contemplating a space on the floor between a dented old birdcage and a pile of mouldy magazines.

"No," she said with a frown. "It's just that when I found Mr Grumpus — the teddy bear, you know — he was sitting right here on a little chair. Now it's gone."

"It's over there, beside the lobster pots," replied John flatly.

Robin looked through the nets, and, sure enough, there was the little chair quite some distance from the birdcage.

"That's odd. Do you think Granny might have come up and moved it?" she asked, then added nervously, "or Milly —"

"No," said John, dismissing both possibilities. "I think it's much more likely you're wrong about where the chair was. This is a strange place because of the nets, and you can easily lose your bearings. I mean — where d'you think that door leads?" he asked, pointing out a barred double door in the gable wall.

Robin hadn't a clue.

"Into another loft?" she guessed.

"Come and see."

John pushed his way back through the nets and Robin followed, hating the way the rough folds swung and caught at her clothes. She was only a couple of steps from the door when John lifted the bar and kicked it open.

As the two halves swung outward, a blast of wet, salty air blew in. To her amazement, Robin saw a rectangle of sky and heard the raucous cries of seagulls as they swooped on the wind. Far below she glimpsed the harbour, and with lurching stomach realised that there was nothing between her and a drop of sixty feet to the quay.

"I told you not to play tricks on me!" she screamed, stumbling back against the nets, which swayed and creaked protestingly in the unaccustomed breeze.

John seemed genuinely concerned.

"Look, I'm sorry," he said. "I didn't mean to play a trick on you, honestly. I just thought you'd be interested. Long ago there was a pulley here to haul the nets up the outside wall. They couldn't possibly have carried them up all those stairs."

Robin didn't suppose they could, nor did she care. Dry-mouthed and dizzy, she watched John grab the lintel, lean out into the rain, and pull the doors shut again. By the time they had made their way back to the landing, Robin had forgotten about the little wicker chair.

9   *The Children's Rooms*

"Shall we look in the attic bedrooms now?" asked John when he had closed the fish loft door. "I am sorry, truly," he added, looking guiltily at Robin's ashen face.

"It doesn't matter," Robin said gruffly. "I'm afraid of heights, that's all."

There was no point, she knew, in telling John that she was even more afraid of Milly Lambert, whose eyes she had sensed watching her ever since she set foot on the stair. He was obviously the kind of person who would never worry about anything he couldn't actually see.

Robin watched cautiously as John opened the first of the bedroom doors; when Milly didn't rush out in a whirl of ectoplasm, she ventured in. The room was small and whitewashed, with a dormer window protruding onto the roof. Its tiny iron fireplace was spattered with the droppings of birds nesting in the chimney, and like the fish loft it was icily — unnaturally — cold. The only furniture was a wardrobe with a discoloured mirror on its door and two narrow bedsteads with damp, striped mattresses folded back on dusty springs.

"Granny told me that the children slept in the attic in Milly's time," said Robin. "I suppose Tom and Robert must have shared this room."

She stood shivering while John stuck his head into the dark wardrobe and felt about inside. A jangling of metal coat hangers made her jump again, and she thought irritably what a waste of time this was. Anyone could see that the room had been stripped and vacated long ago. She was opening her mouth to say, "Come on, I'm frozen," when John uttered an exclamation.

"Wait a minute! I've got something!" he squawked.

It sounded so dramatic that Robin gasped in anticipation, but anticlimax followed. John's find was nothing but a grubby grey woollen scarf. A cloud of dust puffed out as he shook it in triumph, and Robin saw that it was peppered with moth holes.

"What a revolting object," she complained, but John had a pleased expression on his rosy face.

"Look," he said, pointing to one corner. "It's got initials on it. 'T.L.' It's bound to have been his, don't you think?"

Robin couldn't help looking with interest at the monogram. "I suppose so," she said. "It looks old enough. But there've been so many Tom Lamberts here, you can't be absolutely sure."

"Well, never mind," said John, putting the horrible scarf round his neck. "At least I've found something." He winked at Robin and added provocatively, "Now, let's see what you can come up with."

Robin made a rude face, but when John breezed out of the room into the one next door, she sighed and followed him.

It was immediately obvious whose room this had been — and, Robin reckoned nervously, still was. The atmosphere was quite different from the forlorn boys' room next door; this one felt like a room which someone had just left — and to which someone might suddenly return. The curtains and carpet were gone, but the pretty rosewood furniture was in good condition. The little bed was covered with a pretty patchwork quilt, and a painting of puppies still hung in its gilt frame above the fireplace.

> *Stockings red, garters blue,*
> *Trimmed all round with silver . . .*

"Did you hear that?" quavered Robin, but when John looked puzzled and said, "Hear what?" she wasn't sure that she had heard it either. But the sense of Milly's presence was stronger than ever, and Robin was sure that she could smell scent. Rose, perhaps — or was it carnation?

While John messed up the bedclothes, Robin hovered in the doorway, feeling as if her heart were in her throat. When he opened the wardrobe and she glimpsed what looked like a headless figure inside, she realised that she was too frightened even to scream. What she actually saw was strange enough. On a hanger, swaying slightly, hung a brown velvet coat with a fur collar and cuffs. Underneath stood a pair of leather boots with rows of shiny buttons. The coat was beautiful and Robin's size; if she had found it anywhere else she would have run to try it on. Instead she stiffened and turned her eyes away.

Seeing Robin's expression, John closed the door. "I'll just have a quick look in the chest of drawers," he said, "then we'll go downstairs."

Robin watched impatiently as he knelt down and began to open and close the empty drawers. Chilled to the bone as well as jittery, she wondered why on earth she had agreed to have anything to do with John's crazy plan.

"Oh, come on," she snapped finally. "Let's go —" Robin broke off abruptly as she noticed the corner of a painted wooden box sticking out from the end of the bed. "No! Wait!" she exclaimed, then wished too late that she had held her tongue.

John whistled delightedly, and seconds later he was dragging the box into the middle of the room.

"It's Milly's toy box," he crowed, and for a moment even Robin forgot her terror in the fascination of handling the toys and laying them out on the floor.

The toys had been well used, but also well cared for — too well cared for, perhaps, since there wasn't a speck of dust on any of them. First out were two rag dolls, then came a yellow spinning top, some wooden skittles, and a marionette. The flatter toys were in cardboard boxes at the bottom of the chest: a game of snakes and ladders, an embroidery kit, two bats and a shuttlecock, a blackboard, and a tin of broken chalks.

"It must've been megaboring before computers," remarked John, sitting back on his heels and surveying the relics of a century back.

But Robin was running a puzzled eye over the toys. "Funny," she said thoughtfully. "I wonder where the skipping-rope is?"

"Eh?" John looked baffled. "What skipping-rope?"

Robin wanted to kick herself. How could she have forgotten to tell him about the letter she had found in Milly's book?

"Come on! I've got something to show you," she squealed.

Leaving the toys scattered on the floor, Robin darted away downstairs with John clattering at her heels. She ran straight to her room and took the fragile sheet of paper from between the pages of *The Magic Fishbone*.

"There now," she said rather smugly, holding it out to John. "That rates better than a manky old scarf, doesn't it?"

10 Milly Waiting

The amazed expression on John's face was deeply satisfying to Robin. So was his ready agreement that a letter in Milly's handwriting was a find far superior to an old scarf. Unfortunately there wasn't time to discuss it just then, because they heard Granny calling them down to lunch.

Suddenly realising how hungry they were, the children tumbled downstairs. They were in the kitchen before John remembered that he was still wearing the scarf. When Granny peered distastefully and said, "What on earth is that?" he decided to take a risk.

"Smart, eh?" he grinned, lifting the drooping fringes and waving them at Granny. "I found it in the attic. Look, it's got initials on it — 'T.L.'. D'you suppose it belonged to the guy whose boat sank in the old harbour?"

There was a tingling silence. Granny paused with the soup ladle poised over the pan and gave John a sharp, warning look.

"It's possible, I suppose," she said repressively. "Or it might have belonged to anyone whose initials were T.L. and who had a dreary taste in scarves.

Now take it off, wash your filthy hands, and remember what I told you."

John winked at Robin and hung the scarf on a hook behind the garden door. When the children had washed their hands at the sink, they sat down at the table. For the next five minutes they ate and Granny read. Then, suddenly, Granny broke her own rule.

"I've just remembered something," she said. "That old scarf put me in mind of it, I suppose. Robert, your great-grandfather, told me once that after the *Milly Dear* went down, Tom Lambert went around all the time wearing a scarf. He wouldn't take it off, night or day, in one of the hottest summers this century. Strange how shock affects people."

"Weird," nodded John.

Granny turned a page and seemed about to go on reading, but instead she looked over her glasses at Robin. "Before we leave the subject," she said, "are you all right, Robin? You haven't heard Milly again, have you?"

"No," said Robin.

In the safety of the warm kitchen, it was possible to believe that she had only imagined Milly's voice earlier in the attic. Milly's invisible, scented presence was something else.

"Fine," said Granny, returning complacently to her book.

John intended to explore more rooms in the afternoon, and as she drank her coffee Robin tried wildly to think of a good excuse for not accompanying him. As things turned out, she didn't need one, because after lunch Granny asked them to help her pack up pottery in the studio. She was so pleased with their efforts that at five o'clock she said she would take them out to supper at the Sandhaven Café.

"Brilliant," said John. "I'm starving again."

The café was a large hut by the shore, decorated with brightly coloured mermaids and crammed with small red tables. Granny and Robin sat down while John hung their wet coats on a row of pegs behind the door.

"I'm so thankful to have all that packing done," Granny said, picking at a fillet of sole while Robin and John tucked into huge platefuls of cod and potato chips. "I need space to sort out my exhibition pieces. The opening's getting too close for comfort."

Robin knew that the exhibition opened next Saturday, because in the afternoon she had seen a poster tacked to the studio wall. It had a picture of one of Granny's sea-blue bowls, and underneath the words:

MARY LAMBERT: RETROSPECTIVE

| The Gallery, Sandhaven | 5 April — 31 May |
| Palmer's Gallery, London | 5 June — 31 July |

Robin was pleased that she would be at Culaloe at the time of the exhibition.

"What does 'retrospective' mean, Granny?" she

asked as she squeezed ketchup on to her fish and chips.

"It means my life's work," replied Granny gloomily. "A way of saying I'm too old to do anything interesting and new."

"I don't believe that," Robin said indignantly. It was just beginning to dawn on her what a distinguished artist her quiet, unpretentious grandmother was. She also thought uneasily of her parents' sour dismissal of Granny's work as "just a hobby."

"Will there be a party?" John wanted to know.

"I'm afraid so," Granny groaned.

Rain had been blowing like muslin curtains from the sea, as they had walked from Culaloe to the café. But when they came out, it was dry, with a full moon dodging among thin, dispersing clouds.

"Perhaps it will be fine tomorrow," said Robin as they walked home along the quay.

"No. It will rain again before morning," predicted Granny, who knew the coast as well as she knew her own kitchen.

While Granny went off to do some more work, Robin and John went upstairs. When he had had his shower, John again came to Robin's room. Together they reread Milly's letter to Tom. It didn't, of course, explain why the skipping-rope wasn't in the toy box; it only confirmed that a skipping-rope had existed.

"There could be several explanations, I reckon," said John. "Milly might just have lost it, or someone at school might've nicked it. Or else, being such a little monster, she might have had another tantrum and thrown it on the fire."

"Not if Tom gave it to her," objected Robin. "But I don't suppose it matters."

Yet for some obscure reason, she thought that it did.

After John had gone off to bed and she was curled up under the duvet with Mr Grumpus, Robin remembered something. When she and John had rushed down from the attic before lunch, they had left Milly's toys strewn all over the floor. Well, Robin thought, if John remembered tomorrow he could go up and put them back in the box. Otherwise, they'd have to stay as they were.

The alarm Robin had felt in the attic had faded somewhat during the day; Granny's calm company was always comforting, and the downstairs rooms at Culaloe were no more scary in daytime than Robin's own home. But now as she lay in the dark, hearing the gurgle of the water pipes and the curious creaks and rustlings of the old house, Robin was again afraid. The certainty that she'd been watched returned to her forcefully, along with the disconcerting feeling that the little bedroom was occupied. Presumably Granny, with her rheumatic knees, didn't go up to dust very often, yet the furniture was clean, and the velvet coat and boots looked as if they had been brushed an hour before. Could a ghost look after her belongings? Robin wondered, biting her fingernail. As well as crying and singing, could Milly actually *do* things?

If Robin could have seen what was happening in the attic just then, she would have had answers to these questions. While she lay in bed, waiting for Granny to come upstairs, the toys in the attic were being tidied away. As the full moon scattered mercury on the black waves and shone coldly in at the attic window, ghostly fingers were lifting the spinning top and the rag dolls and laying them carefully on top of the box of snakes and ladders. Pale and insubstantial in the moonlight, Milly Lambert ran bloodless hands over her precious playthings and muttered crossly to herself.

How dare they touch her toys, these horrible children with their ugly clothes and loud voices? How dare they steal Tom's scarf that she had given him the Christmas before — But there. She wouldn't think about that. All the toys were safe now, except for her skipping-rope and —

Oh, except for her favourite toy, the teddy bear that Papa had brought her from Glasgow, with a little chair for him to sit on, so long ago. Milly had only left him in the fish loft for a moment, and when she returned that girl had stolen him. But Milly would get him back. Yes, and she would punish the girl, just as she always punished people who annoyed her. Horrid Robert, and the son he'd dared to call Tom . . .

Milly rose up in the cold moonlight and drifted sadly to the top of the attic stair. Should she go down now, she wondered, find the girl and scare her witless? She was pretty scared already, thought Milly, with a thin, sneering laugh. It would only take a moment to wreck her completely and snatch Mr Grumpus back. She was so lonely up here without him. So lonely . . .

Milly sighed and whimpered a little in self-pity, but it was so long since she'd been downstairs that she was almost as afraid of the living as they were of the dead. Besides, there was no hurry. Milly decided that she would wait a little. Then when she had made herself angrier and stronger, she would go down, take back her teddy, and make those nasty children sorry.

11   *Robert Lambert's Desk*

Granny had been right about the weather. Towards morning, a cloud from the west rolled over Sandhaven and unfurled itself across the sea. Robin was jerked awake more than once by the foghorn braying like a lost animal, and when she got up it seemed as if the house were wrapped in fleece. At breakfast, Granny looked sympathetically at the children.

"I was thinking," she said, "that on days like this you might like to use the upstairs sitting room as a den. There's a television and some games in the cupboard that used to belong to your parents." She smiled and added, "I always feel guilty when my guests don't get sunshine on their holidays."

"That's a great idea. Thanks," said John warmly.

Robin was surprised by his enthusiasm, but as they tidied up the kitchen, he explained.

"We need a base for our operations," he said, "and that sitting room will do nicely. Besides, there's a desk there that we should investigate."

Robin wasn't sure about that.

"I don't think we should poke about in other people's desks, John," she objected. "Dad would go into orbit if Tom and I touched his."

But, as usual, John had an answer. "That's different," he said. "Your dad probably keeps his bank statements in his desk, and bills he wouldn't want you to see. It'd be wrong to rummage in Granny's desk, but the one upstairs isn't hers. It belonged to old Robert Lambert, and he's been dead for years." When Robin still looked unconvinced, he urged, "Oh, come on, Rob. How are we ever going to find out what really happened on the *Milly Dear* if we don't grab opportunities like this?"

So Robin capitulated, for three reasons. Firstly, because if she refused, John would go ahead without her. Secondly, because she remembered that Granny had told her to do as she liked. Thirdly and most persuasively, because if they were busy in the sitting room, John wouldn't suggest that they continue searching in the cold, haunted rooms up above.

The sitting room was next to Granny's bedroom. It had the half-resigned, half-expectant atmosphere common to rooms which were once the hub of a house but are now rarely used. It was full of dead people's belongings, uncomfortable furniture, heavy ornaments, and oil paintings reflecting the Lamberts' long bonding with the sea. The large television in the corner was like an intruder from an alien world.

The mahogany desk which interested John stood between two windows curtained with lace and snuff-coloured velvet. When he had switched on the electric fire, he made straight for the desk and opened the lid. Robin looked wearily at pigeonholes stuffed with notebooks and sheaves of paper secured with rusty paper-fasteners and red thread. She noted un-enthusiastically that there were three deep drawers below.

"This will take for ever," she said.

For a while, Robin's misgivings seemed justified. Sifting through piles of business letters addressed to "Robt. Lambert, Esq." of "T. Lambert & Son, Sandhaven Fisheries", the children began to despair of finding anything remotely connected to the mystery of Tom and Milly's last voyage.

The drawers were filled with grubby manilla files and account books, some dating back to the middle of the nineteenth century. Lunchtime came and went before they had thumbed through all of them. Robin was bored stiff and even John was looking glum as, in the middle of the afternoon, he heaved out the bottom drawer. Then, suddenly, their per-serverance was rewarded.

"Look!" exclaimed Robin, peering into a dusty cardboard carton.

John scrambled towards her and was leaning over her shoulder as she tipped the contents onto the dark red carpet.

"At last," he said, with a satisfied sigh.

It was clear that their great-grandfather had wanted to assemble some mementoes of his dead brother and sister. There were two tiny envelopes, one marked "Tom" and the other "Millicent", each containing a wisp of colourless baby hair. There was a school magazine dated 1908 in which Tom had a little article entitled "My Dog Rusty", and a programme from a school pantomime in which Milly had played an elf. More sombrely, there was a faded newspaper cutting telling of the mysterious accident in which Milly Lambert had lost her life, and a letter from the War Office in London dated 30 April 1915. Formal and comfortless, it regretted to inform Mr and Mrs Thomas Lambert that their son was "missing, presumed killed" in battle near Ypres.

"What a load of tragedy for one family to bear," said Robin. "Two children lost and their poor old father in bed after a stroke. It's all so sad."

John didn't reply. He had picked up two old photographs mounted on gilt-edged card, and was staring at them with both fascination and repulsion.

"Here — look at these," he said, pushing them over to Robin.

One photograph showed Tom, Robert, and Milly sitting on a bench in the garden at Culaloe. Milly sat between her brothers, a dark-eyed, pouting child in a lace-collared smock and a straw hat. Robert stared woodenly at the camera, looking faintly absurd in a short-trousered sailor suit. Only Tom, in his stiff white shirt and tweed jacket, looked happy. Bright-eyed and curly-haired, he sat up straight and twinkled at John and Robin as if they were his friends. That was what made the other photograph so shocking.

In it Tom stood alone against a wall, a forlorn, shrunken figure in breeches and a buttoned-up army tunic. His bright smile had vanished, along with most of his hair. From a thin, haggard face, his dull eyes stared despairingly. It was difficult to believe that he was only sixteen.

Robin's eyes filled with tears. Even John was moved.

"Poor guy," he said thickly. Then he added without thinking, "You'd think he'd seen a ghost."

12   A Horrible Discovery

Not surprisingly, Robin didn't sleep well that night. All evening she had been fighting back tears; by suppertime her head ached, and it had been sweet relief to get into bed and switch out the light. But even though she was exhausted, sleep wouldn't come. Tossing and tangling in her duvet, she heard the grandfather clock strike every hour from eleven until three before she fell into a light, restless sleep.

Strange dreams culminated in a dreadful nightmare. Robin was in the garden, playing a skipping game with Milly, while Milly's brother Tom dozed on a bench nearby. But the skipping-rope turned into a thin green snake which jerked away from the girls and whipped towards Tom, raising its flat emerald head to strike. With a scream stuck behind her teeth, Robin started up in bed. She was shaking from head to foot and her body crawled with sweat and fear.

Eventually she did sleep again, but all through the night she seemed to hear Milly's song above the purling waves:

> *Stockings red, garters blue,*
> *Trimmed all round with silver . . .*

69

Because she hadn't heard Milly for sure since her first night at Sandhaven, Robin managed to convince herself in the morning that the singing had been part of her dreams. Still, she got up feeling scared as well as tired. Not for the first time, she wished that she had refused to pry into the old tragedy. But it was too late for wishing now. At breakfast, it was obvious from John's heavy eyes that he hadn't slept well either. He didn't say so, but at the table he suggested that since the weather had improved he and Robin should have a day out.

"We can take the bus along the coast to Wellbank and go swimming at the Leisure Club," he said. While Granny was in the pantry, he added, "We need some time away from here."

Robin agreed. Granny found her a swimsuit, saying humorously, "In this house we have everything," and gave John money for their bus fares and lunch. "Get the four-fifteen bus back," she said as she waved them off, "otherwise you'll have to wait till after five."

With a feeling of release, John and Robin climbed the Seagate, Sandhaven's principal street, to the bus stop on the main road. The morning sun glinted on the sea, and the wind, having blown the rain clouds away, was now busy drying the roofs. Looking down the steep hill to the harbour with its pleasure boats and towering steel crane, Robin could see the long chimneys of Culaloe rising into the pale sky. Suddenly she was overwhelmed by the contrast between the unremarkable fishing village and the haunted house at its heart. As she clambered into the squat country bus, Robin had the weird feeling that perhaps everything that had happened to her since she had come to Sandhaven was a dream.

In the cheerful, humdrum surroundings of Wellbank Leisure Club, however, Robin was relieved to find that she could shelve ghostly matters for a while and have fun. She was an excellent swimmer, much better than John, which secretly pleased her. While John swam doggedly up and down the pool, practising his strokes, Robin dived and somersaulted and darted like a fish under the warm turquoise water. Her pleasure was only spoiled once, when it crossed her mind how different it must have been for Tom, battling through the cold water towards the breakwater, and for Milly, screaming and floundering in her long skirt and petticoats as the boat pushed her down remorselessly into the inky sea.

After swimming, John and Robin ate hot dogs and drank Cokes in the cafeteria overlooking the pool, then spent time in the gym while they waited for the bus. Trundling back along the coast road, they felt relaxed and rather drowsy. Once out of the bus they set off down the Seagate, swinging their swimming bags and looking forward to tea and cookies by the kitchen fire. Something very unexpected was to happen, however, before they reached Culaloe.

Emerging onto the quay between the old and new

harbours, John and Robin were intrigued to see a small crowd gathered around something lying on the harbour wall. They were surprised to see Granny, wearing her tweed jacket over her pottery apron, in conversation with a man in blue dungarees and a red baseball cap. The expression on her face was so serious that Robin feared there had been an accident.

"Granny!" she called, running across the quay.

Granny looked down at her, then at John's questioning face.

"It's all right," she said reassuringly. "This is my friend Mr Lindsay. He's in charge of the dredging here." Her next words hit the children like a punch. "Half an hour ago he came to tell me that the crane has brought up the wreck of the *Milly Dear*."

Robin began to tremble violently, but she managed to catch hold of John's sleeve. When he began to push his way through the huddle of onlookers, she followed him.

What remained of the *Milly Dear* lay in a pool of dirty water, giving off a dank, unwholesome smell. Mr Lindsay's workmen had hosed it down, and Robin thought that it looked like a black skeleton with a knobbly backbone and thin, broken ribs. Most of the planks had been stripped away by sea creatures, but you could see the stump of the mast, broken off most likely as the upturned vessel hit the seabed, and one rust-eaten rowlock still jammed into the rotting wood. The rowing bench was gone, but the stern seat was intact, as was the stern itself. That, thought Robin with revulsion, must have been where Milly Lambert had been sitting just seconds before her death.

"I suppose it definitely is the *Milly Dear*?" she whispered, wishing there could be a shred of doubt.

John nodded and pointed to the stern. It was still possible to make out a few ghostly letters: M LL DE SAN VEN.

Suddenly Robin felt so dizzy that she thought she was going to faint. There was a high singing in her ears, drowning the soft lapping of black water against the quay.

"Are you OK?" asked John anxiously, putting out his hand to steady her.

"Yes, I'm OK," said Robin, as the world stopped spinning and the sky settled down again. "It's horrible, though, isn't it?"

"Gruesome," agreed John.

The little crowd of sightseers dispersed quite quickly. The wreck wasn't very interesting to people who had never heard of Milly and Tom. Granny accompanied Mr Lindsay into his prefabricated office further along the waterfront. John and Robin were left alone by the shell of the *Milly Dear*.

"We're not going to find any clues here, worse luck," sighed John. "All washed away by the sea."

"I suppose," said Robin, not caring much.

When they saw Granny come out of the office and say goodbye to Mr Lindsay, Robin and John ran to meet her. Robin took her hand and they walked silently home together under the evening star.

As Granny, Robin and John approached Culaloe, it didn't occur to any of them to glance up at the window of Milly's room. If it had, they might have glimpsed a pale, frowning little face behind the glass. Disembodied as she was, Milly knew what had happened on the quay. Now, as she watched the moon rise over Barns Island, she was a-shiver with loneliness and pain.

Turning away from the window, the little ghost curled up on the bed where she'd slept when she was alive. Concentrating very hard, she began to conjure up scenes and people of long ago. Still hurtingly familiar after so many years, they formed on the moonlit wall then faded, like old photographs exposed to the light.

Sometimes these shadow companions comforted her, but not now. With the wreck of the *Milly Dear* lying like a dark stain on the harbour wall, she couldn't control them. Terrible memories of that last day came flooding back. Milly shrank in horror from the flickering images of joy, betrayal, and death.

"Oh, Tom," she sobbed. "Why did you leave me? Where are you? Why don't you come home?"

There was no answer, but Milly heard a door opening down below. The warm, intimate voices of the living sounded in the old house. One was the voice of the girl who had stolen Mr Grumpus, another of the boy who was her friend. The jealousy she had always felt for the friendships of others gnawed inside Milly like a dull pain.

I'm upset, she thought, and remembered how Mamma had always said that Milly mustn't be upset, because that made her angry, and then she did bad things. Fretful as she was, Milly couldn't restrain a smirk at the memory of silly Mamma, who had been so afraid of the bad things Milly might, and often did, do. But being angry had always made Milly strong, and strength rose in her now.

It was time to start teaching those children downstairs a lesson. Milly would begin as she always had with people who annoyed her, by teasing them for a while. Then when she was bored with teasing she would stage — what had it been called in that stupid pantomime where she'd wanted to be Cinderella and had been given the part of an elf? — Yes, of course. A grand finale.

Down in the kitchen, Granny was taking off her jacket and hanging it up behind the garden door. "Well, well, what an unpleasant surprise," she said grimly.

Robin and John nodded.

"What will happen to the wreck?" asked John.

"Joe Lindsay's brother owns the *Jenny Spinner*," Granny told him. "Joe's going to ask him to take the

Milly Dear out to sea and sink it off Barns Island. It should have a decent burial, don't you think?"

Then before either of the children could speak, she put her hand into her apron pocket and took out a tubular object about the length of a child's hand. Like the ribs of the *Milly Dear,* it was coal-black, and Robin caught a whiff of the same undersea smell.

"What is it?" she asked.

Granny wrinkled her long nose fastidiously as she held up the thing to the light.

"Joe called me into his office to give me this," she said. "He mistakenly thought I'd be interested. Apparently it was stuck under the stern seat in the *Milly Dear* and fell down when the workmen hosed away the mud."

She laid the workmen's find gingerly on the log basket and rubbed her fingertips on her apron.

"But what is it?" repeated Robin.

"It's the handle of a child's skipping-rope," Granny replied.

13 Bad Saturday

On Saturday morning John was loading the dishwasher in the kitchen when he heard Robin yelling upstairs.

"John! John, please come! There's a flood in the bathroom and I don't know what to do!"

John dropped a handful of cutlery into the basket and galloped upstairs to find Robin standing barefoot in a pool of water on the landing.

"Brilliant," he said heavily.

"I must've left the tap running and the plug in the basin when I went down to breakfast," sobbed Robin. "I've turned the tap off, but there's water everywhere. Granny will be furious."

"No, she won't," John said reassuringly, but when he opened the bathroom door and wildly foaming water swirled out to meet him, he rolled his eyes in disbelief.

"Do you always put bubble bath in the washbasin?" he asked, and to Robin's chagrin burst out laughing.

"Of course not," she snapped. "There must've been soap on the floor."

Yet when John had fetched mops and old towels

from the broom cupboard downstairs and she was paddling about trying to dry the bathroom floor, Robin couldn't help glancing at her bottle of bubble bath on the glass shelf. She could have sworn that last night it had been half full. Now it was almost empty. But because she couldn't bear to contemplate another explanation, Robin told herself not to be silly. Lack of sleep must be making her absent-minded.

It took more than an hour to restore the bathroom to normality, squeeze out the mops, and hang the towels out to dry in the garden. Robin was grateful to John for helping her — and not telling her what a fool she was. Even Tom would have been exasperated at having to spend an hour on Saturday morning clearing up a mess Robin had made.

"Fancy going for an ice cream?" she asked as they came back upstairs. "My treat," she added.

But before John had time to answer, there was a loud crash just above.

"What the hell?" exclaimed John, taking the last few steps in one bound. He threw open the door of his room, and Robin heard him groaning loudly. "Oh, no!"

"What is it? What's happened?" she gasped, running in behind him. She nearly fell over John, who was squatting by the bed and picking over the shattered remains of his tape recorder.

"I must have left it too close to the edge of the table," he said regretfully. "Probably the curtain blew in and knocked it off. Doesn't seem to be our day, does it?"

Robin looked at the billowing blue curtain and the tiny table crammed with John's tapes, paperbacks, comics, and alarm clock. Yes, she thought, John was right. It was just another unfortunate accident. But why was she suddenly so cold, and why was there a faint, familiar scent on the landing?

"Do you smell anything?" she asked John.

"No," he replied. "Let's go for that ice cream now."

So Robin ran to her room to fetch her purse, but the morning's troubles weren't over yet. At the top of the stair a thread caught her foot, and with a scream she tumbled head over heels down into the hall.

"I've broken my leg!" she howled. "I've broken my arm!"

Granny, summoned by a panicking John, kept her own alarm well hidden.

"You really should be more careful," she said in the brusque tone grown-ups often use when children have frightened them. But she knelt beside Robin on the floor and ran gentle fingers over her arms and legs, bending her joints and examining her head for bumps. "You'll live," she said eventually, helping Robin to her feet. "And cheer up. If you'd been my age, you'd have broken your neck."

To Robin, who couldn't imagine ever being Granny's age, this was no comfort. Later, after John had gone to fetch the ice cream and they were eating it in the sitting room, she said what she really thought.

"I don't believe it was an accident. I think Milly Lambert tripped me."

John, who had started twiddling the controls on the television, turned round with a startled expression.

"Oh, come on, Rob. Be serious," he said. "There's a loose strand in the carpet at the top of the stair. Granny's just told me to take scissors and cut it out. Besides, Milly isn't that kind of ghost."

"Isn't she?"

"No. She sings and she cries — according to you and Mum. But there's no evidence she's ever done anyone any harm."

Which was all very well for him, Robin thought sourly.

After lunch, John found a cardboard box in the kitchen cupboard and brought it up to the sitting room.

"This is our file on the case," he said, rather pompously, as he wrote "Lambert and Lorimer, Private Detectives" on the lid with a felt pen.

Robin, who was still shaken after her fall and not in the best of moods, watched unenthusiastically as John put into the box Milly's letter, the old scarf, and Robert Lambert's mementoes of his brother and sister. But when he took the handle of Milly's skipping-rope out of his pocket, she couldn't help protesting.

"How disgusting! I thought Granny had put that thing in the garbage can." She grimaced.

"So she did, and I took it out again," said John. "It's evidence."

"Is it?"

"Yes. It's evidence that Milly took the rope with her on the day she was drowned," insisted John.

The last thing Robin wanted was another conversation about Milly, yet she couldn't help responding.

"That doesn't really mean anything," she said. "Milly had just recently got the skipping-rope from Tom — "

"Had she? How do we know that?"

Robin was surprised that he had to ask.

"Because it's here, in the letter," she replied, taking the yellow sheet from the cardboard box. "On 5 June 1914 Milly thanked Tom for the postcard and the skipping-rope, and asked him to hurry home from London because she was looking forward to their sail to Barns Island."

"Oh, I see. You think it was *that* sail she was talking about," said John thoughtfully. "That she drowned on the way back from Barns Island."

"It seems likely, doesn't it?" asked Robin. "The accident happened on 13 June, according to Milly's tombstone. That was only nine days later, and meanwhile Tom had to get back from London."

"Clever you," said John admiringly, and for a moment Robin felt quite pleased with herself. "I assume she just took the rope with her," she went on, "the way you cart something round when you're pleased with it."

"Right." John leant over and took the letter out of Robin's fingers. There was a pause while he scanned it. "I wonder why Tom was in London?" he mused.

Robin shrugged. "On a holiday, probably. That's why people go to London," she said flatly. Her moment of triumph over, she slumped back into her former mood. "Does it matter why he was in London?" she said fretfully. "Does it matter that Milly took the rope with her in the boat? We're no closer to finding out how the accident happened, are we?"

"Then we must find another clue," insisted John. "We're doing this for Tom Lambert's sake, remember."

His high-mindedness was getting on Robin's nerves. She resented knowing that John was really enjoying himself. Soon, however, that was to change.

14 The Magic Lantern

"Listen," said John at breakfast on Sunday morning. "Have either of you seen my pocket diary? I thought it was in my rucksack, but it isn't, and I can't find it anywhere." When Granny and Robin both shook their heads, he blew out his cheeks in dismay. "Mum will freak out if I've really lost it," he said. "It has my school bus pass in the cover and my tickets for the library."

Robin tried to look sympathetic, but she had troubles of her own. All night long she had been disturbed by Milly Lambert's voice piping in the wind and had dreamed of drowning and falling through doors that opened treacherously out on the sky. Now her eyes felt as if they were full of sand, and her egg tasted like nothing at all. She was too tired to worry about what had happened to John's diary, and even when, later in the morning, a red-hot coal landed on the hearth rug and almost set fire to the kitchen, she hardly had the energy to help John stamp out the flames. But again Robin smelt a stale, sweet scent and felt a cold draught blowing across the floor.

The early morning had been bright, with the sound of church bells gusting on the breeze. But by lunchtime it was raining and the light wind had risen to a howling gale. From the sitting room windows, John and Robin watched clouds of spindrift whirling above the seething waves.

"What a hell of a place this is," growled John. "When I grow up I'm going to emigrate to California."

"Who would blame you?" Robin said.

They spent the afternoon with the light on, lolling in front of the television. *The Last of the Mohicans* was showing, which would have been fine if the television hadn't seemed to be on the blink. At every exciting moment the screen went blank, the light cut out, and the bars of the electric fire faded. But the minute John got up to investigate, everything came on again.

"A gremlin," he said.

"Name of Milly," muttered Robin, but John only laughed.

At six o'clock, when the film was followed by a programme of hymn-singing from an old people's home, Robin grabbed the remote control and zapped it. She felt annoyed because, as usual after a weary day, she was waking up towards evening.

"Didn't Granny say there were some games in the cupboard?" she asked. "Fancy a stupendously exciting round of indoor golf?"

John made a face, but he got up and went to open the cupboard beside the fireplace. Most of the shallow shelves were packed with gardening catalogues and paperback books, but on the two bottom shelves there were games in battered boxes: draughts, *Scrabble, Monopoly.* There was also a square black metal contraption with an electrical flex wrapped round it. John lifted it onto a small table in the middle of the room and dusted it with his handkerchief.

"What d'you think this is?" he asked.

Robin leant on the table and considered.

"It's a sort of projector," she said, pointing to a brass-bound lens which poked out from one side. "There's a slot for putting in the slides. But why has it got a little chimney on top?"

This question was answered by Granny, who had come to warn them that supper was almost ready.

"You've found the old magic lantern," she said, coming in and sitting down by the table. "I'd forgotten it was here. The chimney was to funnel off smoke from the kerosene that was originally used to light it up."

"Who did it belong to?" Robin asked.

"Goodness knows." Granny shrugged her shoulders. "To some nineteenth-century Tom, I dare say. It was wired for electricity when your grandfather was a boy, and your parents used to play with it on rainy days."

"Why is it called a magic lantern?" asked John.

"I believe the first ones invented were used by magicians to create optical illusions," Granny replied. "People who didn't understand the mechanism thought they were seeing ghosts."

Robin shivered, but the others didn't seem to notice.

"I wonder if it still works?" said John.

"Plug it in and find out," suggested Granny. "If it does, you'll find a box of slides in the bottom of the cupboard. Supper in five minutes."

When Granny had gone downstairs, John unwound the flex and plugged the magic lantern in at the wall. A bulb flicked on inside and a pallid square of light was projected onto the wall. Robin found a long wooden box full of glass slides, their edges bound with sticky black tape. But before they could slot one into the lantern, Granny called them down to supper.

"Never mind," said John as they went downstairs. "We'll have something to do between supper and bedtime."

"Would you like to see a slide show?" Robin asked Granny as they ate sausages and baked beans.

Granny shook her head regretfully. "I'd love to," she said, "but Mr MacNab from The Gallery is coming in to finalise details of the exhibition. Only six days to go, and I'm getting nervous. Thanks all the same."

"You'll miss a great show," said Robin, more truthfully than she knew.

"Do you want to put the slides in?" asked John, when they were back upstairs.

"No, thanks. I'll be the audience," said Robin, trying to get comfortable in a rock-hard armchair.

"OK." John slipped a slide into the slot and

pushed it experimentally to and fro. "I'll put out the light, then."

Like many nineteenth-century families, the Lamberts seemed to have had a passion for having themselves photographed. One after another, grainy black-and-white images appeared on the wall. There were pictures of nameless men with whiskers and gold watch chains, and stiffly dressed women with hats like baskets of fruit. There were shots of children building sand castles, fishing in rock pools, and riding donkeys on the beach.

Marginally more exciting were pictures of the Lambert fishing boats, the *Highland Mary* and the *Star of the Sea,* with bearded crewmen in peaked nautical caps. But after an hour Robin was yawning and John was again muttering about the tediousness of life before computers and heavy metal.

"Why don't we pack this in and see if there's anything decent on the telly?" suggested Robin, but John said, "In a minute. There are only three slides left. We might as well run them through."

"If you like," Robin agreed.

She was leaning back in the armchair with her eyes half closed when she heard John make a sharp, exploding sound with his lips. A moment later she was sitting bolt upright, her attention riveted to the picture on the wall.

Robin and John saw Tom and Milly Lambert standing outside the front door of Culaloe. Tom, grinning widely under his mop of curly fair hair, was wearing an open-necked shirt and dark trousers. Milly, in a white summer dress with a low-slung sash and sailor collar, had a straw hat perched on her dark ringlets. She carried a rug over her left arm and in her right hand she clutched a skipping-rope.

"Do you think they're going where I think they're going?" asked John hoarsely.

"Yes," Robin said.

John pushed a little handle on the magic lantern and the slide disappeared. With trembling fingers he put in another.

"We're right," he breathed.

The second picture showed a view of the harbour wall. Milly and Tom were on board the *Milly Dear*. Sitting in the stern, with the picnic basket under her feet, Milly was waving and looking as pleased as punch. Tom was standing in the bow with a coil of rope in his hands.

They looked so cheerful, so innocent of the trag-edy about to overwhelm them, that Robin could scarcely bear to look. She shivered violently, but not only with the sense of doom. Despite the central heating and the electric fire, the temperature in the sitting room seemed to have dropped below zero.

"John," whispered Robin. "Is there another slide?"

"Yes." John was shivering, too. "Do you want —"

"I think we should," Robin replied.

At first it seemed that the final slide was blank. Although the square on the wall darkened slightly, no image immediately appeared. Then something utterly weird happened.

As if a dense fog had thinned, the *Milly Dear* again came into view. Her sails were furled and Tom Lambert was seated at the oars. But the oars were flailing and the boat was tilting dangerously. Numb with horror, John and Robin saw Tom's face dark, his eyes bulging and his lips stretched over his teeth in a hideous grin. Behind him stood Milly, hatless and dishevelled, with her skipping-rope wound tightly round his neck. With a look of murderous fury on her tearstained face, she was trying to strangle Tom.

In the same instant that the fog closed over this unspeakable scene, a low moan told Robin and John that they were not alone. With a smell like dry rose petals in their nostrils, they saw the ghost of Milly Lambert in the middle of the room. Grey and faded as an old photograph, she stood in her pleated smock and lace collar, thick woollen stockings and buttoned ankle-boots. On her face was such a look of terror that for a moment Robin actually wondered if she was afraid of them.

But Milly, who had come downstairs to fetch Mr Grumpus and had been drawn by the sound of voices in the sitting room, wasn't even looking at John and Robin now. She was staring at the square of light where her own anguished memories, triggered by the sight of her father's old magic lantern, had just betrayed the last secret she and Tom had ever shared.

15   One Piece Missing

"But why on earth would Milly do such a thing?" Pale and bewildered, Robin sat up in bed while John hugged his knees at the other end. "She loved Tom. Why would she want to kill him?"

John shook his dark head. The colour was returning to his cheeks and he had stopped shaking, but as Milly had faded through the closed sitting room door the boy whom nothing would frighten had been very frightened indeed. Robin couldn't help feeling a grim satisfaction as she remembered his trembling lip and staring eyes. It served him right, she thought, for being so cocky.

Robin had been frightened too, but she had already had days and nights of hearing Milly and sensing her presence. Seeing the ghost hadn't been a lot more scary than not seeing her but knowing she was there. It was the disclosure of Milly's crime that made Robin feel sick. It was gruesome almost beyond belief, but the ghastly expression on Milly's face had confirmed that it was true.

"At least we know why Milly took her skipping-rope with her on the boat," said John, trying to reassert himself.

Robin looked startled.

"You mean that she took it deliberately, intending to murder Tom?" she asked. "Oh, surely not, John!"

John blinked, taken aback by such vehemence. "What other explanation is there?" he said.

Robin frowned. "Well, like I said before," she said, fumbling for the right words, "she took it because it was a new present and she was pleased with it. But when she quarrelled with Tom on the boat and saw red, she used the rope because it was there. We know she had a terrible temper. Granny told me that her rages were famous. I reckon she lost her cool about something and went for Tom in a blind rage. I don't think it was premeditated."

John rested his chin on his knees and thought about this.

"She said in her letter that she'd like to kill Robert," he pointed out.

Robin shrugged. "I know. But you can say that kind of thing without really meaning it," she said.

John, who had occasionally been guilty of such remarks himself, was silenced for a moment. Then he said, "Only of course she didn't kill Tom."

"No. I suppose he beat her off and the *Milly Dear* keeled over in the struggle," said Robin, shuddering as she visualised the tragedy unfolding in the silent, fogbound sea. "By the time he got free of the rope and stopped choking, it would have been too late to rescue Milly. No wonder he didn't want to tell anyone what had happened."

John nodded, then clicked his fingers. "Of course," he said. "That explains the scarf, doesn't it?"

"What about the scarf?"

"Remember," said John. "The day I found the scarf, Granny told us that after the accident Tom Lambert went around with a scarf on. She said he wouldn't take it off even at night. She thought he was in shock, but the poor guy was really wearing the scarf to hide the marks of the rope on his neck."

"Yes," said Robin, automatically putting her fingers to her throat. "You're right, of course. It all fits."

"A lot of it does," agreed John. "It's like a jigsaw puzzle. Only there's still one piece missing."

"Which piece?"

"The piece that would tell us why Tom and Milly quarrelled so violently," replied John. "We can't ask Granny. She said I wasn't to mention Milly to you again, and if she knew what's been going on she'd go bananas. But I was thinking . . . Mum might know. Robert Lambert was her grandpa, and she used to chat with him a lot when she was young."

"Aren't your mum and dad still away?" asked Robin.

"No," said John. "They must've got back from the convention last night. Why don't we go out to Clunybank tomorrow and talk to Mum? She'll be dying to meet you anyway."

When she'd had time to think about anyone but Milly Lambert, Robin had longed to meet Aunt

Miriam too. But she still looked uncertainly at John.

"Will your mum believe us?" she asked. "I mean — we only know what happened from the picture on the wall, and —"

"And what?"

"Well, it was just spooky," said Robin. "No one could possibly have taken such a photograph. I don't think the picture's on the slide at all. I think it had something to do with Milly being in the room. If I'm right, there's no proof, is there? Your mum would think we were making it all up."

John knew that there was an easy way of finding out whether there was a picture on the slide, but wild horses wouldn't have dragged him back to the sitting room that night.

So he said, "We don't have to tell Mum about the slide. We'll just say we found some papers, which is true, and got interested in the story. If she tells us anything useful, great. If not, there's nothing lost."

"OK," Robin agreed.

"Then I think I'll go to bed," said John. "Will you be all right?"

Just for a moment, remembering the whey-faced scaredy-cat he'd been earlier, Robin was furious. But she was too tired to snarl at him.

"I'll be all right," she said. "Somehow I don't think we'll hear from Milly again tonight. She's got other things on her mind."

*   *   *

Robin was right, although not in the way she thought. When Milly had fled in tears from the sitting room, she had met someone on the attic stair. He had been looking for Robin, but he was a kind person, and when he saw Milly's distress he went upstairs with her and tried to comfort her. In the unexpected joy of companionship, Milly forgot about teasing Robin and John, and getting back her teddy, and her plan for a grand finale.

16   The Old Tin Box

At half-past ten the next morning, Robin and John were once again at the bus stop. They were waiting for the bus that passed the end of Clunybank Road on its way from Wellbank to St Andrews.

It was an overcast, blustery day, and Robin huddled morosely under the fibreglass shelter. She had enjoyed a night of uninterrupted and dreamless sleep, yet had got out of bed feeling anxious and depressed. The events of the previous evening were vivid and, perversely, the memory of Milly's ghost was more frightening in daylight than it had been in the dark. For the first time since she had arrived in Culaloe, the sound of the sea was getting on Robin's nerves.

John had met a school friend in the Seagate and sat with him on the bus. Robin sat alone on the landward side, watching seagulls skimming the furrows just as they did the waves. It seemed there was no getting away from the sea.

Still, it was a relief to escape the haunted rooms of Culaloe for a while. The children got out of the bus at a hamlet called Clunywell and began to plod inland down a narrow, grass-verged lane.

Clunybank was visible from a long way off, and Robin could see why it was worth a lot more money than Culaloe. The large old farmhouse sat confidently among the fields, its back protected by a scarf of evergreens. With its peach walls, white sash windows, and faded pink tiles, it looked quite disdainful of the brash modern farm buildings surrounding it.

"Nice place," remarked Robin. "It must be good knowing it'll be yours one day," she added to make conversation.

She was amazed when John made a rude noise.

"Except that it won't," he said. "Oh, that's what Mum and Dad would like, but I have other plans. I told you yesterday. When I leave school, I'm going to California."

Robin squinted sideways at John's red-nosed, defiant face.

"I didn't think you were serious," she said.

"Well, I am," John assured her. "Last year we went on holiday to San Francisco, and I fell in love with the place. My uncle Harry, my dad's brother, owns a hotel there. I'm going to work for him and train to be a chef."

"And are your mum and dad — er — agreeable?" asked Robin.

John gave a sudden snort of laughter.

"Agreeable? They're spitting teeth," he said. "Especially since my big sister Valerie's already pushed off to Australia. But Granny supports me. She says nobody should have to be a farmer just because their old man owns a farm."

Robin admired determined people who knew how they wanted to spend their lives. She hadn't a clue what she'd do when she grew up.

Whatever Aunt Miriam thought of John's plans, however, she gave him and Robin a warm welcome.

"I was going to 'phone and ask if you wanted me to fetch you over," she said. "I'm glad you just decided to come."

Sitting by the fire in the warm farmhouse kitchen, Robin wrapped her cold fingers round her coffee mug. What wouldn't Mum give for a place like this, she thought, eyeing the blue ceramic tiles and expensive pine furniture. Robin wasn't envious, but it was clearer to her than ever why her father was sick at being left out of his grandfather MacIvor's will. But she liked Aunt Miriam, a rosy woman in old cords and a green sweater, who didn't overwhelm her with anxious hospitality. In that way, Robin reckoned, she was like Granny.

Aunt Miriam had brought presents from Birmingham, where the farmers convention had been held. There was a box of fishing flies and a baseball cap for John, and pink satin slippers for Robin.

"They're lovely. Thanks," said Robin.

She really did like the slippers and hoped she sounded grateful enough. But today she couldn't even enjoy an unexpected present properly. Her attention kept wandering as she saw again and again in her mind the terrible picture of Milly trying to murder Tom. Robin wondered how on earth John was going to get any information out of Aunt Miriam without telling her a lot more than he wanted her to know. But as it turned out, he didn't even have to try. Amazingly, Aunt Miriam took the initiative.

"Listen," she said suddenly, after they had toured the farm and were having lunch at the kitchen table. "When I was at the store in Wellbank this morning I met Amy Halligan from Sandhaven. She told me that the old harbour coughed up the *Milly Dear* last week. Did you see it?"

"Yeah, we saw it," John told her through a mouthful of hamburger. "It gave us the creeps. You're too late to see it, though. The *Jenny Spinner*'s dumped it out at sea."

"Thank goodness." Aunt Miriam winced and wrinkled her nose. "I hate wrecks," she said, "and when I think of that poor little Milly. . ."

"Robin's heard Milly at Culaloe, just like you," John told her, avoiding Robin's eye.

Aunt Miriam nodded. "Yes, Mother told me," she said. "I hope you're not scared, Robin?" Robin shook her head untruthfully. "Because there's no need. Milly's never done anyone any harm."

Robin had been convinced that if she heard this complacent and now ludicrous remark once more, she'd scream. Now, somehow, she managed not to. Before she could say anything, however, Aunt Miriam went on.

"It was really odd hearing about the *Milly Dear* being found. I hadn't thought much about Tom and

Milly for ages. Then just before we went away to Birmingham, I found something at the back of the hall cupboard that brought it all back to me."

"What was it?" Robin asked, somehow managing to sound quite cool.

"It was an old tin box from Culaloe," Aunt Miriam told her. "It used to be in Grandpa Robert's desk, and I must have brought it when I moved here — probably because I liked the picture on the lid. I don't remember ever opening it before, though."

Robin saw John swallowing hard, but he managed to sound cool, too.

"Anything in it?" he inquired.

"I'll show you," Aunt Miriam replied.

While she was out of the kitchen, John and Robin puffed out their cheeks and rolled their eyes impatiently. The suspense was dreadful. After an agonising delay, Aunt Miriam came back carrying a small tin box with a picture of lambs on the lid. As she prised it open, John and Robin almost fell over each other scrambling to look.

At first glance the box seemed full of rusty paper-fasteners, pen nibs, and perished rubber bands. But when Aunt Miriam had tipped these out, she took from the bottom a piece of printed cardboard and a folded sheet of paper. It was grey and powdery, and was obviously another letter. Aunt Miriam spread it on the table so that John and Robin could read it. Once again, they could scarcely believe their eyes.

THE GREAT WESTERN SHIPPING
COMPANY
HEAD OFFICE : 23 GOLDEN COURT, LONDON
W.C. 2

8 June 1914

T. Lambert, Esq.,
Culaloe,
Sandhaven, Fife.

Dear Sir,

I am pleased to confirm that, following your interview last Friday, we have decided to offer you a position as clerk in our New York office at a starting salary of $400 *per annum*. A passage has been booked for you on the SS *Sherman,* sailing from Southampton on 20 July. You are requested to take up your duties on Monday 3 August. Your ticket and documents are enclosed.

Yours faithfully,
J.M. Reid (Director).

"Mum," said John, his eyes almost out on stalks, "did you know that Tom Lambert was planning to go to the United States?"

"I have a vague recollection," replied Aunt Miriam. "Maybe emigration runs in the family," she added, giving John a wry smile.

Robin was too astounded to say anything. She picked up the ticket that would have taken Tom Lambert to a new life in America and turned it over in her hands. It was the last piece of the puzzle, and it made the whole picture horribly clear.

Of course, Robin thought, Tom had arranged the sail to Barns Island as an opportunity to tell Milly that within weeks he would be going thousands of miles away from her, perhaps for ever. Robin imagined the outward voyage under the sun, with Milly happily chattering and completely unaware of the bombshell her favourite brother was preparing to drop. They would have landed on the island and had their picnic, Tom wondering nervously when the best time would be to break his news.

Perhaps he had funked it, because surely it had been on the return trip, when the cold haar had already rolled in and Tom had taken to the oars in the becalmed water, that he had finally told his sister the truth. Then Milly, enraged by fear of loss and a sense of love betrayed, had lost control. Robin could almost hear her words, flung against the silent wall of the mist.

"I'll kill you for this . . ."

Robin's reverie was interrupted by the arrival of John's father. She was jerked out of the past to shake hands and chat to a kindly, fair-haired man in a checked shirt and green quilted jacket. Out of the corner of her eye she saw John pick up the letter and the ticket and put them in his pocket.

"You don't mind if I take these to show Granny?" he asked his mother deceitfully.

"Not at all," Aunt Miriam replied.

It was three o'clock when Aunt Miram said that if the children wanted a lift back to Sandhaven, they'd have to go.

"My holiday's over and I have to get back to milk my cows," she explained. While John was upstairs collecting some extra clothes, she said gently, "Robin dear, is there any news of your brother Tom?"

Robin shook her head. "Not really," she replied. "He's still unconscious and the doctors don't know whether he'll get better or not."

"I'm so sorry," Aunt Miriam said.

There was an awkward little pause, of a kind Robin had got used to. To fill it and ward off further questions which would upset her, she remarked, "You know, Tom would love it here. He wants to be a farmer when he grows up."

The response was astonishing.

"Does he really?" said Aunt Miriam. "Well, when he wakes up, ask him if he'd like to come and work at Clunybank. Uncle Jim and I are going to need someone to help us in our old age, when our son's in California and our daughter's in Western Australia."

"Thanks. I'll ask him," Robin said.

17 Bad News

That night in the sitting room, John laid out on the hearth rug the contents of his cardboard box. When he had added the letter from the shipping company and the one-way ticket to New York, it was possible to trace the terrible chain of events that had ruined two young lives.

Milly's letter and the handle of the skipping-rope she'd taken on the fateful voyage to Barns Island. The three scary magic lantern slides. The scarf Tom Lambert had used to disguise the red marks of the rope on his neck. The horrifying photograph of the young soldier who had abandoned his plans to emigrate and had gone to war instead. The story was compelling, but there was a problem. Robin, who had first recognised it last night, returned to it now.

"We know what really happened," she said, "and as far as we're concerned Tom Lambert is completely in the clear. But we'll never be able to convince anyone else, unless —"

"Unless what?" John said uneasily.

Robin lifted a glass slide from the rug and ran her fingers over its dark surface.

"Unless this slide always shows the attempted murder," she said. "And there's only one way to find out."

"I suppose," said John, glancing nervously at the magic lantern, which still stood on the table in the middle of the room. He had no desire to provoke another ghostly appearance. Then he caught Robin's challenging eye and felt his reputation for boldness slipping still further away from him. "OK. I will if you will," he agreed.

But although both children had to summon courage to slip the slide into the lantern, to Robin at least the result was almost a foregone conclusion. Not only did the fog on the wall fail to part, but the slides showing Tom and Milly's departure for Barns Island had also gone blank. Milly didn't appear in the sitting room either, which Robin thought proved her point.

"It's as I thought," she said. "We saw these pictures because Milly was looking over our shoulders last night. They were in her mind, not on the slides at all."

John had already come to the conclusion that Robin was a smart kid, but he wasn't going to swell her head by telling her so. Instead he said, "Never mind. Maybe it would be enough for Tom that we know the truth." He paused, then added more in hope than conviction, "Maybe it's enough for Milly, too."

Robin reckoned that this was unlikely. Remembering the grey, distraught face staring at the sitting room wall, she just couldn't believe that they'd heard the last of Milly Lambert.

For the next three days, however, it seemed that perhaps John was right. As March had become April, winter had given way to spring. The sun glittered on the sea. Late crocuses in the garden crumpled, while the chrome-yellow spears of the daffodils tilted and began to burst. Granny sent her best dress to be dry-cleaned and Robin decided what she was going to wear to the opening of the exhibition on Saturday evening.

Most pleasantly, nothing ghostly happened. Although John's missing diary hadn't turned up, nothing else disappeared. There were no mishaps and Robin slept well, undisturbed by dreams or voices. The children played outdoors, and when they returned the house seemed blessedly empty. Relaxed and enjoying life at Sandhaven, Robin was thinking less and less about what might be happening at home. Then, in the middle of supper on Thursday evening, the telephone rang.

Aunt Miriam quite often 'phoned in the evening, and when Granny went into the hall to answer, Robin thought nothing of it. When Granny came back, however, both children knew that something was wrong.

"John, dear, make yourself scarce," Granny said. "I want to talk to Robin."

"It's Tom, isn't it?" whispered Robin as John, looking stricken, left his bacon and egg and departed without a word.

"Yes."

Granny sat down at the table and clasped her thin

hands under her chin. She looked intently at Robin with her dark eyes.

"Is he dead?" Robin asked, scarcely able to believe that her lips were forming such a question.

Granny shook her head.

"No," she said, "but there's a change in his condition. Your mother was ringing from the hospital. She thought you ought to know."

"What kind of change?"

"Apparently Tom has become very hot and restless, but they can't get him to wake up." Granny was obviously distressed, but she went on speaking calmly. "He keeps struggling to get out of bed," she told Robin, "and he cries out that he doesn't want to leave Culaloe."

"Leave Culaloe? But he isn't at Culaloe," said Robin, bewildered. "He doesn't even know I'm here."

"My dear," said Granny gently, "no one knows what goes on in the mind of someone as sick as Tom. The point is that Mum and Dad want you to be prepared for bad news. Tom's doctors don't think this is a good sign."

"Should I go home?" Robin wondered.

"Not right now. Mum's going to ring again when there's something new to tell us."

Like that he's died, Robin thought. Suddenly she wanted to be by herself for a while.

"I'll go to my room," she muttered, and ran out of the kitchen and up the stair.

On the landing a blast of cold air rushed past her, stirring the curtains and lifting the edges of the rug.

18   A Question of Ownership

Robin had never really believed that the discovery of the truth about the boating tragedy would silence Milly Lambert for good. Yet it seemed unbelievably cruel that, just when she was so desperately unhappy about her brother, the malicious spirit should begin to haunt her again.

> *Stockings red, garters blue,*
> *Trimmed all round with silver,*
> *A rose so red upon my head*
> *And a gold ring on my finger . . .*

Plaintive and mocking by turns, the childish words of Milly's song disturbed Robin's night. When she did sleep, she dreamt of Tom with his bandaged head and of falling through doors that led to nowhere. Awake, Robin felt dazed and sick. The thought of the rest of her life without Tom was intolerable, yet she now believed that that was what lay ahead of her. She could live to be as old as Granny and never see Tom again.

Friday was a dreadful day. On her way up to clean her teeth after breakfast, Robin was sure she saw a whisk of white petticoat and a black buttoned boot disappearing round the curve of the stair above. In the bathroom she found her toilet bag thickly smeared with toothpaste both inside and out. As she stood staring in disgust, a howl of rage from John's room made her drop the bag and rush to see what the matter was.

"That mean little pig's cut the sleeve off my sweater!" roared John, holding up the ruined garment.

There was no longer any pooh-poohing, Robin noted grimly, of Milly's ability to do people harm.

When she had scrubbed her toilet bag and John had hidden his vandalised sweater for fear of Granny's seeing it, the children went for a long, silent walk along the windy shore. When they came back, John discovered that his comics had been torn to shreds. Robin, changing out of her boots in the hall, found her shoes filled with water.

"How can we stop her?" she groaned despairingly.

"We can't," said John.

All the same, they spent a boring afternoon on the landing, guarding the doors of their rooms. Milly, of course, did not appear.

For Robin, however, the worst fright of the day came in the evening. She had washed her hands and was crossing the landing to go down to the kitchen for supper when suddenly she heard a giggle she seemed to recognise. Turning sharply, she could have sworn she saw feet scampering up the shadowy stair. Not Milly's feet, but feet in silly cat slippers, with an inch of thin leg between them and bright red pyjama bottoms.

Robin wouldn't have believed that there was a level of terror which she hadn't already experienced, but she now realised that there was. Sweating and shaking uncontrollably, she clung to the banister at the top of the stair. She wanted to run to Granny, sob out the whole story, and beg to be taken home. She knew that Granny would believe her, but — into her spinning head came a cold, rational thought — her parents would not. Spending all their time at Tom's bedside, they would be outraged by what they'd see as attention-seeking on Robin's part. Besides, telling Granny would get John into dreadful trouble and, apart from Tom, John was now Robin's best friend. So she pulled herself together somehow, went down to the kitchen, and said nothing. As she forced down her supper, she tried to convince herself that she must have been wrong. Tom's peculiar remark about staying at Culaloe was making her imagine things.

The party to celebrate the opening of Granny's exhibition was scheduled for seven-thirty on Saturday evening. On Saturday morning, Mr Grumpus disappeared. When she went down to breakfast, weary-eyed after yet another disturbed night, Robin had left him sitting up against the pillow. When she returned to make her bed, he was gone. Mr Grumpus had been a great comfort to Robin in these last difficult days, and losing him was the last straw. Sitting down on the bed, she burst into tears.

John, coming up from the kitchen, heard her crying and came to find out what was wrong.

"Milly Lambert's taken Mr Grumpus," sobbed Robin. "Why does she have to be so horrible?"

John felt desperately sorry for Robin and blamed himself bitterly for starting something which he knew was now out of control. But although in one way he regretted his arrogance, in another he longed to do something to restore his image as a strong, fearless sort of guy. He made a quick decision.

"Don't cry, Robin," he said. "I bet you anything you like she's taken Mr Grumpus up to the attic and hidden him in her old room. I know you're too scared to go up there again, but I'll go. Don't worry about a thing."

Robin herself had thought that she was too scared to set foot in the attic again. But even in her present distress she reckoned this was the most conceited speech she'd ever heard. Her hackles rose, and so did her courage. She wiped her eyes and blew her nose.

"I am not too scared," she said with dignity. "Anything you can do, I can do, you pompous twit."

It was one of the nice things about John that he could laugh at himself.

"Ouch!" he said. "Sorry. Shall we go?"

"I'll put on my cardigan," Robin said.

She was glad, a moment later, that she was wearing something warm. As she and John mounted the gloomy stair, each landing was damper and chillier than the one below. By the time they reached the attic, Robin's teeth were again chattering with cold and apprehension. What an ass I am, she thought. I should have let John come alone. What am I going to do if Milly's in her room?

John too was shivering and his rosy cheeks were tinged with purple. Secretly he was having the same thoughts as Robin. But with his self-esteem already so badly dented, he couldn't retreat. Taking a deep breath, he forced himself to swagger forward and throw open the door of Milly's room.

There was a waft of Milly's stale scent, but mercifully no grey figure rushed to meet them. Yet even as she sighed with relief, Robin had a sense of not seeing what she expected. Then she realised why. The toys, which she and John had left all over the floor last week, had been put back in the box. Robin had no doubt who had tidied them. Her eyes moved from the closed toy box to Mr Grumpus, who was smiling benignly in his little chair by the empty hearth. She also saw the little blackboard from the toy box, propped against a leg of the chair. On it, in red chalk, were scrawled the words, GRUMPUS IS MINE. LEAVE HIM.

"How stupid of me," exclaimed Robin, suddenly understanding. "Of course Mr Grumpus must have been hers. Granny told me he was about ninety years old. That's why Milly's been getting at me, because I took her bear."

"Then why has she been getting at me?" demanded John indignantly.

"Maybe she doesn't like your face," said Robin, grinning faintly. That a ghost could be jealous of the friendship of the living never crossed her mind. Robin looked round the room in a kind of helpless bafflement. "But how can she?" she wondered. "Move things around, I mean?"

"Poltergeists do," pointed out John. "They can smash china and move furniture. It was on the telly once. And I read somewhere that spirits can write messages."

"This one can," agreed Robin, again reading Milly's abrupt order.

"So what d'you want to do about Mr Grumpus?" asked John. "We'll take him, if you like. We could smuggle him out to Clunybank and leave him in my room till you can take him to Inverness."

Robin hesitated. She really liked Mr Grumpus, and the temptation to grab an opportunity to pay Milly back was strong. But she knew that it simply wasn't worth the risk.

"Thanks, but no," she said. "Just think what that maniac Milly might do when she found he was gone. I'll leave him."

But she minded losing Mr Grumpus and turned quickly away.

"Right," said John, hardly able to hide his relief as

he followed Robin out onto the landing. "I'll make her a present of my diary as well. Now let's go and —" He broke off suddenly as he noticed the expression on Robin's face. Her eyes were stretched with alarm and every drop of colour had drained out of her cheeks. "What is it, Rob?" asked John, squinting at her anxiously in the dusty light of the landing window. "Are you ill?"

With a trembling finger, Robin pointed to the fish loft door.

19   Come and Be Killed

The fish loft door was half open, which it certainly hadn't been when John and Robin had come upstairs. The fishy stench of the old nets drifted out onto the landing. But that wasn't all. As the sound that had alarmed Robin reached his ears too, John suffered the same sense of stupefaction. He heard a high-pitched giggle, then voices and the soft padding of feet.

"You can't catch me!"

"Oh, yes I can."

"Come on then, Milly. Try!"

There was squealing and more giggling, then: "Come on, Tom. I want to show you something. Over here!"

John's legs were shaking so much that he had to lean against the wall. He stared at Robin with his mouth open and felt his heart thumping as if he'd just run a mile.

"Tom?" he whispered thickly. "Her brother? Then he's come back."

"No," said Robin. "My brother Tom."

Somehow the goggling incomprehension on John's face helped to clear her mind. Remembering

Tom's strange remark about staying at Culaloe, and the slippered feet she'd glimpsed on the stair last night, Robin accepted something ineffably strange. While Tom's body lay in a hospital bed in Inverness, his spirit had come to Culaloe. Perhaps he had come to find Robin. Instead he had found Milly Lambert — or she had found him.

"Well, she can't have him," vowed Robin, anger suddenly making her strong. "He isn't her brother. He's mine."

Gritting her teeth she pushed past John and stepped into the fish loft.

Once over the threshold, the first things Robin noticed were light, movement, and air. It was momentarily confusing, since the fish loft was normally so stuffy and dark. But then, looking down a corridor between two rows of creaking, swaying nets, she saw that the door that had featured in so many nightmares was open. Robin saw sunlight and spinning rain and heard the voluble sea.

"Tom!" she called. "It's me, Robin. Where are you, Tom?"

But the words were muffled by the nets, and there was no reply. Holding her breath, Robin moved on tiptoe down the corridor towards the open door. She heard John's footfalls at her back, but just now his nearness didn't matter. The battle for Tom was between Robin and Milly alone.

As she emerged into the space between the nets and the door, it was Milly whom Robin saw first. The ghost-girl was standing with her back to the racing sky. In her filmy grey dress, black stockings and boots, she teetered jauntily on the sill, tossing her curls and beckoning with thin, long-fingered hands.

"Come on, Tom," she was saying encouragingly. "Don't be scared. Come and play with me."

Robin watched without moving as Tom came out of the shadows and stood a few paces from the door. It tore at her heart to see him, a pale, insubstantial creature with a scar on his forehead and huge blue eyes under his fringe of reddish hair. Suppose, she thought, that she was too late — that he was dead already? But she pushed that dreadful idea away from her and said again, "Tom! It's me, Robin."

Tom stood awkwardly in his red pyjamas and furry slippers. With a slight smile on his curly lips, he looked uncertainly from Milly to Robin, then at Milly again.

"Come and see the harbour, Tom," wheedled Milly. "Come and see the boats and the seagulls, and let me teach you to fly."

To Robin's horror, Tom took a hesitant step towards the door. Screwing up her courage, she leapt out and confronted Milly Lambert.

"You can't have him," said Robin clearly. "He isn't yours, he isn't dead and he won't come and be killed."

Milly gave Robin a mocking glance but didn't even bother to answer. She again concentrated on Tom.

"Come on, Tom," she coaxed, as if he were an

infant afraid of the deep end of a swimming pool. "It's quite safe. Just come and stand by me."

Tom shuffled closer to the door.

Then Robin knew, as clearly as if a voice were speaking into her mind, that Tom stood on a knife-edge between life and death. If his spirit were enticed through the open door, far away in Inverness his heartbeat would fail and the beeping machine fall silent. She wouldn't let that happen.

"Tom," she said urgently. "Don't listen to her. She's a ghost, and she wants to make you a ghost, too. Stay with John and me, and we'll have such fun together. John lives on a farm, and Aunt Miriam says you can work there when you leave school. Please don't go with Milly. You're not the Tom she wants at all."

There was a pause, which lasted for perhaps ten seconds, although to Robin it might have been ten hours. Tom stood almost on the edge, the wind lifting his fine hair. He looked at Milly and Robin with perplexed eyes.

"Come, Tom," wheedled Milly, again holding out her pale hand.

Then Robin did the bravest thing she would ever do in her life. Willing Milly not to touch her, she stepped between Tom and the void. She heard the mewing of the gulls and felt the sweat and sickness of vertigo but didn't allow herself to look down. With her heels over the edge and the wind snatching at her legs, she grabbed Tom's shoulders and thrust him back against the nets.

A sensation like an electric shock ran up Robin's arms. She felt some substance under her fingers, different from flesh and bone. In the instant when Tom smiled and disappeared, John stepped forward and grabbed Robin. A hiss of fury and disappointment came from Milly's lips, but by the time Robin had recovered enough to turn round, she too was gone.

Far away downstairs, the telephone rang.

20 The Opening of the Exhibition

During the rest of that day, Robin was so happy she thought she would never be afraid again. The morning telephone call had confirmed what she already knew in her heart, that Tom had regained consciousness and was going to live. When she spoke to Mum on the 'phone in the afternoon, it was to hear that Tom's feeding tube had been removed and that he had swallowed a little soup.

"Has he said anything?" Robin asked.

"Yes." Mum sounded vaguely puzzled. "He's still talking about Culaloe. He think's he's been there with someone called—Molly, was it? Now he wants to know how soon he can join you there."

"Maybe something just told him I'd gone on holiday without him," said Robin, thinking how feeble these words sounded.

She was thankful when Mum said lightly, "Yes, who knows? The unconscious mind or something. Anyway, it doesn't really matter."

Granny, when first told that Tom was going to recover, had been quietly but obviously happy. Yet when Robin relayed to her the news that Tom was longing to join her at Culaloe, Granny had looked . . . "shifty" was the word that occurred to Robin.

"We'll have to think about that some other time," she said.

Robin would have been hurt if she hadn't known that, with the opening of her exhibition only three hours away, Granny had other things on her mind.

At six o'clock Robin went upstairs to change into her best skirt and blouse. When she reached the landing, she was sure that Milly was half way up the next flight of stairs, watching her through the banisters. But instead of being nervous, Robin now felt gleeful.

Looking up into the shadows she said, "I know you're there, Milly, but you don't scare me any more. Tom's getting better. I've won, and there's nothing you can do."

There was no hiss of annoyance, not even a starchy swish of petticoat in reply. The rambling house remained silent apart from its usual sea-echoes and windy rattlings. Robin smiled triumphantly and went into her room.

At seven o'clock Uncle Jim and Aunt Miriam arrived to take Granny, John and Robin to the Sandhaven Gallery. Aunt Miriam brought eggs and a large plastic container of homemade soup.

"In case you all fancy a quick supper when you get back," she said.

Chattering and laughing, John and Robin tumbled out of the house. Robin leapt into the back of the car while John waited for Granny to lock the door. When she'd got in, he squeezed in beside her and banged the door shut. Uncle Jim started the engine and the car moved off along the quay.

From the high window of her room, Milly Lambert watched the family group depart. She was quivering with painful emotions; fury because Robin and John had pried into her private affairs and found out what happened on the *Milly Dear,* jealousy because they were so happy together, and grief because she had lost her new friend.

Tears ran down the ghost's cold cheeks as she remembered the boy she'd called new Tom. Of course he hadn't been the Tom she really wanted, but he'd been so friendly and funny in his red suit and ridiculous slippers. For a while they'd been having such fun that Milly almost forgot the children downstairs. But when new Tom had started to talk about his sister Robin, and Milly had realised that he meant the girl who had taken Mr Grumpus, jealousy and the desire for revenge had clawed inside her again. When she understood that Tom was not yet dead, she had seen a triumphant opportunity to achieve two ends at the same time.

While new Tom was playing with the toys, Milly had crept downstairs and done more spiteful things, laughing when she saw how upset Robin and her friend John were. But not half as upset as they will be, she had thought gleefully, when she had lured new Tom through his life's final door. Only it had all gone horribly wrong.

Resting her icy forehead against the glass, Milly sobbed bitterly. It was so unfair. A moment more and she'd have made new Tom hers for ever and ever, but that interfering Robin had had to arrive and — yes, Milly had to admit it. Robin's love for her brother had been stronger than her own malice and selfishness. So Robin had won. But if Robin really thought there was nothing Milly could do, she had a surprise coming.

The last of the daylight was like a scatter of silver coins on the sea. The moon glinted on the cold rocks of Barns Island and the Sandhaven fishing boats put quietly out to sea. Milly stood staring until the lights dwindled among the stars. When she turned from the window there was a strange smile on her face.

"Well, old friend," she said to Mr Grumpus. "It's good to have you back, but I must leave you for a while. It's time for the grand finale."

At the Sandhaven Gallery, Robin and John were finding the opening of Granny's exhibition a sad disappointment.

"Not exactly a rave, is it?" grunted John, when he ran into Robin outside the washrooms.

"Gruesome," agreed Robin.

The children looked glumly through glass swing doors at the crowd of mostly elderly people in stuffy suits and tight dresses. Jostling and squawking, they slithered on the highly polished floor. Occasionally some of them would glance at Granny's beautiful work in the illuminated cases around the walls, but Robin guessed most of them had come for the free wine and canapés. Granny, like a long-legged, exotic bird in her iridescent black dress and silver jewellery, stood twiddling the stem of her wine glass and glancing surreptitiously at her watch. Robin knew that she was desperate to get home and go to bed.

"Why were these freaks invited?" Robin asked indignantly. "Don't tell me they're Granny's mates."

"No way," said John. "Granny doesn't have mates. It's a case of 'Have money, buy pots', I reckon."

This reply puzzled Robin. Granny didn't seem to her the kind of woman who cared about money. She didn't drive a new car or wear expensive clothes or even go to the hairdresser.

"Does selling her work matter a lot to Granny?" she asked.

John shrugged. "It mattered a lot when she started the pottery," he said. "When our grandfather was drowned, Granny discovered that the *Highland Mary* wasn't properly insured. The *Star of the Sea* had to be sold to pay off debts, and Granny desperately needed money to bring up her kids. I reckon she sells now because people want to buy."

"So — is she quite well off?" Robin asked.

John grinned. "She doesn't actually *have* to dress out of jumble sales and drive an eight-year-old Ford banger," he replied. Then he amazed Robin by adding indiscreetly, "Mum says Granny wants cash to leave to your dad when she snuffs. She thinks he was robbed over Clunybank."

Robin was speechless as she remembered the mean things Dad and Mum had said about Granny. She hoped that when they found out the truth, they would be ashamed of themselves.

By nine-thirty the party was thinning out. By a quarter to ten only a few flushed and giggly guests remained, having their own party in a corner of the room.

"I'm shattered," Granny said inelegantly to Uncle Jim. "Round up the sheep, James. We're going home."

Five minutes later they left the brightly lit gallery and drove home in the dark, enjoying the moon and stars. Uncle Jim dropped Granny and the children at the bottom of the Seagate, tooted his horn, and took off along the waterfront. Granny found the front door key in her bag and put it into the lock.

"Well, thank goodness that's over," she said, switching on the hall light.

She stopped so suddenly that John, who was right behind, banged into her and nearly knocked her over.

"What's wrong?" he asked, startled.

"Oh, God! We've been burgled," Granny groaned.

21　The Grand Finale

As she stepped into the hall, Robin gazed round at a scene of wreckage. Drawers from the hall chest had been emptied on the floor, the umbrella stand was overturned and coat hangers were strewn everywhere. But although the telephone had been ripped from the wall, Robin was in the kitchen before it dawned on her that the intruder had really had vandalism in mind.

The damage and mess were stunning. Every plate and bowl on the dresser had been smashed to smithereens. Shards of sea-coloured pottery covered the floor. House plants had been torn from their pots and earth scattered everywhere. Aunt Miriam's soup and eggs were dripping thickly down the pale blue walls.

"I'll look upstairs," said John, but Granny stopped him.

"Stay where you are," she ordered harshly.

Too shocked to argue, John obeyed. Granny went to check the back door and the ground-floor windows. No locks had been forced, nor panes broken.

"Our visitor didn't come in downstairs," said Granny. "If he came over the Fergusons' roof, he may still be in the house."

"Should we call the police?" quavered Robin.

"It seems we have no telephone," replied Granny brusquely, "and the nearest police station is at Wellbank. Anyway, I can handle this myself." In alarm Robin watched her lift the poker from the hearth and close her fingers tightly round the handle. "You two are to stay here," she ordered, "until I get back."

"Forget it," said John violently, picking up the tongs. "There might be a maniac up there with a gun."

"Oh, rubbish," snapped Granny. "This is kids' stuff." But she looked at John as if he had grown without her noticing. "All right," she said. "Only don't do anything stupid."

"I'll leave that to you," promised John, with a last spurt of impudence.

The joke was mistimed. Granny gave John such a ferocious glare that he flinched and Robin burst into tears. This had been the longest, most stressful day of her life and she didn't think she could take any more. But when she saw that Granny and John were paying no attention, she wiped her eyes and followed them upstairs. Anything seemed better than being left alone in the vandalised kitchen.

Forgetting her rheumatic knees in her indignation, Granny went straight to the top of the house. John followed her up the attic stair, but Robin held back. Biting her fingernail, she crouched on the moonlit landing below, listening to John's and Granny's footsteps overhead. Her earlier confidence gone, Robin was once more afraid of ghosts.

It seemed ages until Granny came down again with John at her heels. He caught Robin's eye and gave a slight shake of his head.

"All clear," he mouthed, as Granny started opening doors round the landing and flicking on the lights.

None of the disused bedrooms on the upper floors had been disturbed, and there was no one to be seen. But John's and Robin's rooms had been attacked; covers had been ripped from the beds, pictures smashed and clothes scattered and torn. Granny's room was untouched.

Up to this point, John and Robin really had thought they were looking for an intruder. But as they glanced round Granny's tidy bedroom, a dreadful thought simultaneously occurred to them. The only rooms vandalised were the ones that they frequented. This attack was aimed at them. As if in confirmation, a trace of Milly's flower scent wafted across the landing.

Before they could do more than exchange horrified glances, however, Granny advanced to the sitting room. Raising the poker, she thrust open the door and switched on the light. With a sinking heart, Robin remembered John's earlier remark about the power of poltergeists.

Even after what they'd already seen, John and Robin were amazed by the savagery of the assault on the sitting room. The books and games from the cupboard lay crushed and jumbled with the papers from Robert's desk, with John's lost diary on top.

Ink had been poured all over them. Ornaments and glass had been shattered and the velvet curtains dragged from their wooden poles. The magic lantern lay dented under the table. Only the television seemed to be undamaged.

The contents of John's cardboard box had been treated with particular venom. The skipping-rope handle had been thrown into the grate and the three slides were pulverised on the hearth. All the paper items were ripped to shreds — apart from one. In despair, Robin looked at the photograph of Tom Lambert in his soldier's uniform, propped up on the mantelpiece. Beside it was the blackboard from the toy box. The message about Mr Grumpus had been rubbed out and a single word chalked in its place. REVENGE.

"The rotten little pig," burst out John indignantly. "We didn't do anything to deserve this."

Granny, who had been standing as still as a stone, came back to life at these imprudent words. As Robin clapped her hand over her mouth, Granny turned to stare first at her, then at John. Robin saw horrified understanding dawn in her dark eyes.

"What exactly did you do?" she asked in a voice as cold as the wind off the sea.

John tried to face up to her, but then he hunched his shoulders and looked at the floor. "It's a long story," he said.

22 Never a Normal Child

Just for an instant, Robin thought that Granny was going to strike John. But Granny rarely did as one expected. Taking the tongs out of John's hand, she said quite calmly, "Listen. First we're going to put the bedclothes back on your beds and get rid of the broken glass. Then we're going to clean up the kitchen. After that, however long the story is, I want to hear it. Understand?"

"Yes," muttered John, while Robin nodded miserably.

It took a long time to remake the beds, hoover up the glass, and sweep into plastic sacks the shards of Granny's beautiful pottery.

"I'm sorry, I'm sorry," Robin kept saying, but Granny was stoical.

"It doesn't matter," she said indifferently. "Fortunately all the pieces I care about are safe in the Sandhaven Gallery."

She seemed to have other problems on her mind.

John, unusually subdued, swept and dusted while Granny and Robin fetched buckets of hot water and did their best to scrub the walls. It was well after midnight when Granny made coffee for herself and cups of hot chocolate for Robin and John. Then she built up the fire.

"I don't approve of late nights for children," she said, "but I don't suppose you're any more ready for bed than I am. I want to know what's been happening, and I want the truth. Start talking."

Robin sat in an armchair and John sat on a stool. Knowing that they had no choice, they took turns telling the story. Robin explained about finding Milly's letter to Tom, and John told about seeing the gravestone and the decision that they wanted to clear Tom Lambert's name. Robin told about the mementoes in Robert Lambert's desk, and how they had puzzled over the question of the missing skipping-rope.

Granny didn't interrupt, but when she heard how Milly had begun to plague them after the raising of the *Milly Dear,* she shivered a little and pressed her forefinger against her lips. When John told about the hair-raising images that had appeared on the sitting room wall, however, she showed no surprise at all. Robin, suddenly thankful to be sharing the burden of knowledge with a grown-up, was eager to tell her about Milly's appearance in the sitting room, but John went rattling on.

"We're sure the pictures told the truth," he said. "Mum showed us a letter she'd found confirming that Tom meant to emigrate to the United States. He even had a ticket to New York."

Granny nodded thoughtfully. "Yes," she said. "I

knew that Tom wanted to emigrate, though I never imagined a connection with the accident. But I'm afraid it's all too probable. Milly was never a normal child. Her rages were pathological, and some of Robert's stories about her behaviour were appalling."

"Such as?" John couldn't help asking.

Granny shuddered. "Such as torturing animals and hurting other children," she said reluctantly. "And she was an arsonist. More than once she set fire to the kitchen, and when she didn't get the principal part in the school pantomime she set Cinderella's costume alight and nearly burned down the church hall."

Remembering the coal that had mysteriously fallen out of the fire onto the hearth rug, Robin, too, shuddered. She supposed they'd been lucky that tonight Milly had decided to break the house up, not burn it down.

"Of course," Granny went on, "Milly was sick. She badly needed psychiatric care, but her father would never admit there was anything seriously wrong. He talked about Milly's 'teasing', and said she'd grow out of it. Her mother was simply out of her depth, and Robert, who had a sweet nature, forgave her everything. Tom was the only person who could control her. But he was young, and no doubt he wanted to see more of the world than Sandhaven."

"He was taking a risk, though, wasn't he?" John frowned. "Taking her out in a boat, I mean. You'd think he'd have realised Milly might freak out when she heard he was pushing off to the States."

Robin nodded agreement, but Granny's mind had evidently moved on to something else.

"Tell me," she said abruptly. "Have either of you actually seen Milly Lambert?"

Robin didn't think that Granny could look worse; she seemed to have aged ten years in the last three hours. But when Robin said, "Yes," her face went even paler and her knuckles whitened as she gripped the arms of her chair.

"Go on," she ordered hoarsely.

So Robin told her how Milly had appeared in the sitting room on the night when the ghostly pictures appeared. She told her about the glimpses she'd had of feet and whisking petticoats, and finally about her encounter in the attic with Milly and Tom.

"I know Milly was out to get me because she thought I'd stolen her teddy," she said, "and I suppose she did mean things to John because he's my friend. But the real fight was about Tom. We saw his ghost, didn't we, John? Only he wasn't dead."

John nodded agreement, but Granny had leant forward in her chair and put her head in her hands.

"Oh, my God," she groaned. "To think of this going on in my house! I should have kept my eye on you, John Lorimer, instead of concentrating on my work and trusting you to do as you were told. When did you ever?" Before John could respond to this bitter question, she went on, almost to herself, "Poor child! Milly Lambert might have been the death of him, but how was I to know? I thought he'd only be in danger if he came to Culaloe."

Robin and John exchanged anxious looks. They wondered whether the night's disaster was affecting Granny's mind. Sensing their alarm, Granny sat up again. She poked the fire, and as the fragile log collapsed in a crimson glow, she pulled herself together. Sitting back in her chair, she began to tell a story of her own.

23   A Dangerous Name

"Robin," Granny began, "you once asked me why I hadn't called your father Tom. I told you I didn't think Tom was a happy name, but that was only part of the truth. By the time Simon was born, I also believed that Tom was a dangerous name — for people living at Culaloe."

"How so?" asked Robin, in surprise.

"Because," Granny replied, "while many people heard Milly Lambert in the house, she only ever appeared when something terrible was about to happen to someone called Tom. Milly's mother was convinced that seeing her ghost caused her father's stroke, and I'm sure that her brother Tom saw her too before he went off to war. I've never seen such a haunted face as in that photograph of him in uniform, and whatever happened to him, his life was ruined. Then there was my young cousin, Tom Mac-Ivor, who came on a visit the year I was married. He was climbing a tree in the garden when a branch broke and he fell, breaking both his legs. When I visited him in the hospital, he told me that just before the accident he'd seen a girl laughing at an upstairs window."

Granny paused, staring into the fire, while John and Robin were lost for words. Presently Granny continued.

"I've never known how often my husband Tom saw Milly," she said, "because he would never talk about her. It was Robert who told me how she'd pestered Tom when he was little, pushing him down steps and hiding his teddy bear. But I do know that just before he put to sea for the last time, the children next door saw Milly at the attic window. They used to ask if the girl upstairs wanted to come out to play. On the night when Tom left Culaloe, never to return, he saw Milly at the window, too."

"How do you know?" gasped Robin.

"I'd gone across the quay with him to say good-bye," Granny told her. "Just before he went on board Tom looked up at the house and said, 'There's that devil's brat at the window, Mary.' It was a beautiful evening with scarcely a breeze and the sky full of stars. But before morning a great storm swept the coast. The *Highland Mary* went down off Inchcape with all hands."

"I think I'm beginning to understand," whispered John, his blue eyes wide with horror.

"Yes," said Granny grimly, "I'm sure you are." But she was looking at Robin as she went on, "When I heard that your parents were going to call their baby Tom, I was appalled. I pleaded with your father to choose another name, but he said I was like a superstitious fisherwoman with my talk of ghosts and omens. So your brother was named Tom, and I knew that however much ill-feeling I caused, I must never let him come to Culaloe."

"Oh, I see," said Robin, understanding at last. "That's why you only invited me when Tom couldn't come."

"Yes. I thought there was no more danger to you than there was to Miriam and Simon — or to any child whose name wasn't Tom. It hadn't occurred to me that this fool John would persuade you to go provoking Milly, or that your brother's spirit might follow you here. When I think what might have happened —"

"Only it didn't," snapped John, offended by her use of the word "fool".

"No thanks to you," retorted Granny.

Robin thought this was unfair. She was sure that Tom's spirit had come to Culaloe because he longed to be there, not because of anything she and John had done. Besides, if they hadn't embarked on these strange adventures, Robin wouldn't have been anywhere near the fish loft when Tom needed her help.

Perhaps Granny understood this too, since she now spoke more gently. But Robin was saddened by her words.

"Worse harm might have been done, I know. Tom is safe, for the time being. Unfortunately, I'll never be able to grant his wish to come on a real visit. Please God, Milly will settle down again now. But while she's here, Toms just aren't welcome at Culaloe."

24 Death in Exile

On Sunday morning, Robin arrived in the kitchen to find Granny looking ruffled and John eating bacon and egg with a mutinous expression on his face. Eight hours apart hadn't eased the tension between them, and Robin realised with embarrassment that she had walked in on a row. As she slipped onto her chair, John banged down his knife and fork.

"You aren't being fair," he told Granny. "I didn't disobey you just for the hell of it. I really cared about Tom Lambert, and the one thing I regret is that the pictures of the picnic day only appeared on the wall when Milly was there. We know what happened, but we can't clear Tom's name publicly. That's a shame."

Now it was Granny's turn to bang on the table. A faint flush rose on her pale cheeks and her eyes were bright with anger.

"What an arrogant wretch you are!" she said vehemently. "Did it never occur to you that Tom Lambert could have cleared his own name if he'd wanted to? He could have shown his parents the marks on his neck and explained why he couldn't save Milly from drowning. Instead he chose to spare their feelings at appalling cost to himself. Do you really think he'd thank you for stirring up this pathetic story after more than eighty years?"

John's face went scarlet and Robin felt herself blushing, too. Although Granny's rebuke hadn't been directed at her, she knew that she was just as guilty as John.

"I never thought of it like that," admitted John sheepishly.

"You never thought at all," retorted Granny. There was an uncomfortable silence while she poured herself another cup of coffee, but then she sighed and said wearily, "Let's leave it there, shall we? I'm so tired of all this."

After breakfast Granny, John and Robin cleared up the mess in the sitting room. Paper, fragments of china, glass and the broken magic lantern were shovelled into sacks and lugged down to the yard. John hoovered while Granny dusted the furniture. Once the job was finished, Granny cheered up considerably.

"I've always hated this room," she confessed, perching on the arm of a chair. "So cluttered with ugly things, but I never felt they were mine to throw away. Now I'll buy a cream carpet and make myself some nice green plates."

Robin cleaned the little blackboard and, with the courage she hadn't been able to summon last night, took it up to the attic. There was no sign of Milly other than a trace of scent, but Robin still experi-

enced the cold and tension that her invisible presence caused. I suppose it will always be like this, she
thought, wondering how on earth it could be explained to Tom that he must never visit Culaloe as
long as he lived.

In Milly's room, Mr Grumpus was sitting on his
little chair by the fireplace. Robin couldn't help smiling at him, but she found that her desire to possess
him had faded. Quickly she put the blackboard into
the toy box and ran downstairs.

During the morning, haze had turned the sun to
a silver, then to a dull pewter circle on the sky. By
lunchtime it had disappeared as the grey haar again
crept softly over the sea. Vapour coiled around the
masts of the boats in the harbour, and the crane was
like a ghostly dinosaur stretching its long neck.

After lunch Granny said that she was going to
take yesterday's newspaper, saved from Milly because it had been left in the studio, and lie down on
her bed.

"After all that's happened, I need a rest," she said.
"What will you do?"

John glanced at the fog-filled window.

"We'll see what's on television," he said. "OK,
Rob?"

"OK," Robin agreed.

So Granny departed upstairs with the paper, and
after John and Robin had tidied up the kitchen, they
followed her. In the strange, bald sitting room, they
switched on the television and tried to make them-

selves comfortable. The scenes of a gangster movie unfolded on the screen, but John closed his eyes and Robin stared without taking in anything that was happening.

Suddenly she felt dispirited. On Tuesday John had to go back to school, and she supposed that since Tom was getting better, her parents would want her at home. Which would be the last she would ever see of Sandhaven and her new friends, because if Tom wasn't welcome at Culaloe, there was little chance that she would be allowed to visit, either. Robin didn't pretend that the events of the past two weeks had been pleasant, but they had certainly been exciting. Now the immediate future, with Tom still an invalid and John far away, seemed flat and uninspiring. At that moment, she wouldn't have believed the excitement that was still to come.

As the film credits rolled, Robin thought she would go to her room for a while. She wanted privacy to have a little cry. But before she could move she was diverted by the sudden appearance of Granny, wearing her dressing-gown and with her hair standing up like exclamation marks all over head. She was brandishing the newspaper, and her eyes and mouth were round with incredulity.

"Come and look at this," she gasped, dropping onto a sofa as if her legs wouldn't support her any more. "It must be him! I mean, it couldn't be anyone else, could it?"

Trying not to laugh, John went to switch off

the television. Robin looked at Granny, uncertain whether to be amused or not. But when Granny jabbed at the newspaper with her forefinger, the children went to look. She was pointing to an item in the section headed *Births, Marriages and Deaths*. When they read it, John and Robin were as electrified as she was.

LAMBERT: At Falmouth Hospital on 3 April, TOM LAMBERT, aged 99 years, of Sandhaven, Fife and Penryn, Cornwall. For 50 years Warden of the Sailors' Refuge, St Michael's Cove.

There was a long silence in the sitting room. Eventually Robin broke it.

"So he didn't die in World War I after all," she said.

"And he didn't come back to Sandhaven. He said he wouldn't," said John.

"He will now," Granny said.

25   A Ghost Comes Home

It was towards evening when a young man came ashore at Sandhaven and walked lightly across the quay to Culaloe. He was wearing sea boots and a dark duffel coat, yet his body seemed to flow with the mist that swirled around his legs and curled softly through his hair. He paused for a moment, looking up at the house, then he opened the front door.

Upstairs in the sitting room, Robin, John and Granny heard the creak of the hinges and the click of the lock. They looked at each other, but no one spoke as feet began to ascend the stair.

At the open sitting room door, Tom Lambert paused and looked in. He had shed his great age along with his body; now he was young and clear and colourless, with tiny pearls of moisture clinging to his curly hair. There was no smile in his eyes or on his full lips, but with a grave inclination of his head he acknowledged the strangers now living in his father's house. Then he continued upstairs. Clenching her hands, Robin counted the steps to the attic. Thirty-eight, thirty-nine, forty, then —

"Tom!" an ecstatic cry rang through the house,

and the listeners below heard the ghostly voices as clearly as if Tom and Milly had been in the next room. "Oh, Tom, I thought you'd never come! I've waited so long."

There was no answering joy in Tom's voice, however. He spoke patiently, but without warmth.

"I know, Milly. I'm sorry. I came as soon as I could."

There was a little pause during which Granny sat with her arms wrapped around her body. John and Robin looked speculatively at each other. When Milly spoke again her delight had faded. A faint note of accusation entered her thin voice.

"I've had such a lot of disappointments, Tom. Other boys with your name have lived here, and every time I heard someone downstairs calling 'Tom!' I thought you'd come home. When I found out that it wasn't you, I was very angry. Then I made bad things happen."

It sounded as though Tom had heard all this before.

"Yes, yes," he said resignedly. "That was always your way, wasn't it? Doing bad things, making bad things happen."

Robin could imagine the scowl these critical words would bring to Milly's face. She wasn't surprised when Milly answered fretfully.

"It wasn't my fault. The children here upset me, and Mamma said I should never be upset. You shouldn't have upset me in the boat, Tom."

Down in the sitting room, Robin and John were aghast at this shameless reproach.

"How can she dare to say such a thing?" whispered John. "She tried to murder the guy, for God's sake."

But Granny, with the air of someone who has just solved a puzzle, said, "Ah! Now I know what's wrong with that child. No matter what she does, she can't feel sorry afterwards."

Tom must have known this better than anyone. Instead of rebuking Milly, he coolly agreed with her.

"You're right. I shouldn't have upset you in the boat," he said. But then he added bitterly, "Fool that I was, I shouldn't have taken you in the boat at all. My mistake was supposing that you would never vent your insane rage on me."

Milly sounded genuinely shocked. "But you were planning to leave me, Tom," she said. "How could you do such a thing? I thought you loved me."

Tom's sigh breathed impatiently through the listening house. "I did love you, Milly," he said. "For all your evil ways, you'd always been affectionate and sweet to me. That was the problem. I could see you were sick and couldn't help yourself, but I knew you'd never be better and I was tired of everyone thinking it would always be my job to look after you. I wanted to be rid of you and have a life of my own. Of course I knew you wouldn't like my going, but I never thought it would turn you murderous."

Milly didn't answer, and kindhearted Robin couldn't avoid a twinge of pity for her. However bad she was, she had waited so long for Tom's return. It must be dreadful to hear such harsh truths. But Robin also winced at the pain in Tom's voice as he continued.

"Only, of course, I could never be rid of you. When I realised that you'd come back to Culaloe and meant to haunt me, I was terrified — so terrified that I ran away and never dared to come home till now. I prayed for death in the war, but though people died all around me, I survived. Still, I covered my tracks, and when it was all over I hoped to slip away quietly and forget. But it was no good. For eighty years, no matter how hard I tried to get rid of my guilt by helping others, I thought of you constantly and blamed myself for the horrible way you died."

Up to this point, Robin had thought that Tom's cruel words were intended simply to punish Milly. Now it occurred to her that what he really wanted was to impress on her that some deeds are too evil to be swept aside and lightly forgiven. The shock of such plain speaking certainly had some effect on Milly, because when she replied the self-righteous whine had gone from her voice. She didn't apologise, but she defended herself with some dignity.

"I didn't come back to Culaloe to terrify you, Tom. I came because I thought you'd be sad without me, and because in spite of what happened you're the only person I've ever really loved. When you ran away, I was brokenhearted. I've been lonely and unhappy, but I never stopped loving you and wanting to be with you again. Now I don't understand why you've come back at all."

"Oh, Milly!" For the first time, there was gentleness in Tom's voice. "Do you suppose I didn't know how sad you were? The most dreadful thing of all for me was knowing that your spirit was haunting our old places, hurting other people because you were suffering yourself. I had to come back, to put an end to all that."

There was another silence, then: "It's the end anyway, now that I know you want to be rid of me, Tom."

The words were bleak, and they must have gone to Tom's heart, because now he answered very kindly.

"I don't want to be rid of you, Milly. I did once when I was young and selfish, but I had a long time for wishing I'd done things differently. Now I'm going to take you away to a place where I can forget and you can learn how to feel. Then generations of children who never knew us can be happy at Culaloe."

"Shall I always be with you, Tom?" The childish voice was full of anxiety and tentative hope.

"Always. Now come." Tom's voice became urgent. "We must find your coat, because it's cold outside and we have a night's sail ahead of us." There was another little pause in which Robin imagined the opening of the wardrobe and the taking down of the brown velvet coat. Then, unexpectedly, Tom laughed. "Don't tell me he's still here! Yes, he can come. But hurry now. Our boat's ready and we mustn't miss the tide."

A door opened up above, then there were again steps on the stair, coming down. This time Tom Lambert passed the sitting room door without a glance, and Milly had eyes only for him. As their footsteps descended to the hall, Granny, John and Robin got up in silence and moved to the window. Robin clutched at Granny's hand.

The mist drifted over the quay like spinnings of fine wool. The harbour lights rubbed through like timid moons. Outside the front door, Tom paused to pull up his hood and draw Milly's fur collar closely round her throat. Then he smiled down at her and took her left hand in his. The three at the window watched as Milly Lambert, with Mr Grumpus in the crook of her right arm, faded through the mist towards the sea.

26 Tom

The most recent Tom Lambert sat on the edge of his hospital bed, swinging his thin legs and looking for the last time at the ward that was more familiar to him than his room at home. Five weeks had passed since he had woken up to learn that, incredibly, he had been asleep for more than three months. He had wanted to go home at once, but had had to stay in the hospital until he had learned to use his arms and legs properly again.

Now, finally, it was time to go. Tom was waiting for his family to come and fetch him. There was a tiny flicker of fear inside him at the thought of the unfamiliar world outside, but mostly he was looking forward to a life that promised to be quite different from the one he had known before his accident.

It seemed that while he'd been in hospital, something that Dad called "mending fences" had been going on. Tom understood this to mean making up old quarrels. As a result, he had acquired new relatives of whom he'd never even heard before. Tonight he would be at home with Mum, Dad and Robin, but tomorrow his aunt and uncle and cousin John were coming to Inverness. They would be bringing the granny whom Tom had only ever met once.

In the evening, there was to be a family party to welcome Tom home. The Lorimers had to get back to their farm, but Granny was staying on for a while. Best of all, when she went back to Sandhaven, Tom and Robin were going with her to spend the summer.

While he was at Sandhaven, Tom was to visit Clunybank Farm and decide whether he would like to work there when he left school. Not that there was much doubt about his decision, Tom thought, grinning to himself. When Dad and Robin had told him that Uncle Jim and Aunt Miriam wanted him at Clunybank, it had been better than twenty Christmas mornings rolled into one.

Yet it was Granny's house, Culaloe, that Tom had always longed to visit. As a little boy he had loved the name, and still when he whispered it he seemed to hear the sea singing inside a shell. The odd thing was that since waking up from his long sleep, Tom couldn't rid himself of the idea that he had visited Culaloe already. Perhaps it was a dream, yet it seemed more vivid than that.

Tom knew that he hadn't seen Granny, but he was sure that he'd played with a girl called Milly. Tom smiled as he remembered how she'd laughed at his pyjamas and furry slippers, but her buttoned boots and stiff petticoats had seemed just as comical to him. Milly had always been singing. How did the song go?

Stockings red, garters blue,
Trimmed all round with silver,
A rose so red upon my head
And a gold ring on my finger.

A nonsense song, but in Tom's memory Milly had been a nice girl. He had enjoyed the games they played in the great windy loft above the quay.

The memory of Milly faded as Tom saw Robin jumping about and waving at the entrance to the ward. As he slipped down from the bed she ran towards him and seized his bag.

"Ready to go?" she asked.

"Ready to go," said Tom.